PERIL en POINTE

A Swan House Ballet School Mystery

Helen Lipscombe

Chicken House

2 Palmer Street, Frome, Somerset BA11 1DS
www.chickenhousebooks.com

First published in Great Britain in 2019
Chicken House
2 Palmer Street
Frome, Somerset BA11 1DS
United Kingdom
www.chickenhousebooks.com

Cover and interior design by Helen Crawford-White
Typeset by Dorchester Typesetting Group Ltd
Printed and bound in Great Britain by CPI Group (UK) Ltd, Croydon CR0 4YY

The paper used in this Chicken House book is made from wood grown in sustainable forests.

1 3 5 7 9 10 8 6 4 2

British Library Cataloguing in Publication data available.

PB ISBN 978-1-910655-79-5
eISBN 978-1-912626-27-4

For my boys

1

The Trouble with the Lilac Fairy

'OK, fairies – one more for luck.' Mr Lamont squints into his phone. 'Can the Lilac Fairy move to the front? And Golden Vine, you to the back. *Milly*, did you hear me? That's it – a bit further back. Smashing. Everyone smile for the camera. Let's hear you say "Scarlet Slipper".'

'Scarlet Slipper!'

'Smiley face, Milly. And again . . .'

'Scarlet Slipper!'

Flash.

Little black spots dance before my eyes.

'Perfect,' says Mr Lamont. 'Let's go, everyone.'

His silvery quiff bobs up and down as he rushes us into the wings of the theatre. 'Now remember what I said, fairies – Enchanted Garden, nice soft arms. Songbird, fluttery hands. Golden Vine, flicky legs . . .'

I inspect my legs. Trembly? Yes. Flicky? No.

'Lilac Fairy, take your ti— Willow, what's the matter?'

Tears pool in Willow's eyes. 'It's no good – I can't dance.' She rubs the scar under her tights. 'It's my leg. It's hurting again.'

Mr Lamont frowns. 'Your leg? But the accident was years ago.'

'It wasn't an accident,' snaps Willow.

The other fairies look at me like they always do. Slightly suspicious and not entirely friendly.

I bite my tongue but the words sneak out between my teeth. 'It *was* an accident, Willow.'

'No it wasn't. You were so mean!'

My cheeks burn. She's right about the last bit.

Mr Lamont pulls a hanky from his navy-blue blazer. 'This is no time for arguments. We can't compete without you, Willow. We need our Lilac Fairy.'

Willow dabs her eyes. 'I suppose the show must go on.'

'She's *sooo* brave,' coos the Fairy of the Songbird.

I sigh and peek around the curtain. I've known Willow Perkins since we were in Ballet Tots. I still remember the smells of angel cake (her) and wee (me) mingling as we did the hokey-cokey. I remember the day she got her scar, too. Willow won't let me forget.

Onstage, the founder of the Scarlet Slipper Ballet Prize nudges her glasses up her powdery nose. 'Your Royal Majesties, my Lords, Ladies and Gentlemen, esteemed Judges. It is my great pleasure to introduce . . .' Dame Anna Popova blinks up at the Royal Box. She clutches her pearly throat. She gasps and drops her speech.

Someone runs on and picks it up. Someone else runs on and runs off again. The audience begins to rustle. When you're 102, people must think you've popovered your clogs every time you reach the end of a sentence.

Dame Anna does a no-need-to-call-an-ambulance-just-yet shake of her wispy, white head. 'Where was I?' she says. 'Ah yes. It is my pleasure to introduce the last of the schools competing for the coveted Scarlet Slipper trophy.'

The fairies crowd behind me and Mr Lamont points up at the balcony. 'Your mother's arrived in the nick of time, Milly. Same seat as usual.'

I beam up at the box next to the royals. Mum's been on tour for three long weeks. I wave into the darkness and Willow does too.

Dame Anna warbles from the stage, 'Dancing the Fairies Variations from *The Sleeping Beauty*, I give you –' she flutters a hand drooping with diamonds – 'LAMONT'S SCHOOL OF DANCE!'

Mr Lamont smiles. 'Off you go, Milly. If you dance half as well as your mother, we're in with a chance.' A little titter passes from fairy to fairy.

Willow gives me a push. I troop behind the Fairy of the Songbird and take my place onstage. The clapping dies. The lights dim. Silence falls over the theatre like fairy dust. The conductor lifts his baton and Mr Lamont holds his breath.

Five minutes later, Mr Lamont breathes out. Four of the fairies have fluttered and flicked without a wobble. The audience is spellbound.

My turn next.

As the music plays, my skin begins to tingle. Who cares about Willow Perkins when you are the Fairy of the Golden Vine! My toes point, my fingers zap, my legs flick. I *bourrée* one way, whirl the other. As I fly across the stage, I wish I could dance for ever, but Willow is waiting. As I curtsey, she whispers behind me, 'Out of the way, Milly. Your mum's here to see *me*, not you.'

Willow Perkins is not a nice person.

Trouble is, I'm the only one who knows it.

As Willow begins to dance, my foot twitches. It inches out. It can't seem to help it. Willow is so close . . . just a bit further and . . .

WHAT AM I DOING? Mum would never forgive me! My foot snaps back, but my legs are tired and I stumble sideways.

Bwmph! Into the path of a twirling tutu.

As the Lilac Fairy crumples, the audience gasps. The lights go up and my eyes shoot to Mum. It was an accident, they say. But Mum's not there. I search for a sparkling tiara, a twinkle of sequins, but I can't see her. I can't see anything – the theatre's too blurry.

Mr Lamont helps Willow to her feet. A bead of sweat drips off the end of his nose. 'Willow, where does it hurt?'

'Everywherrrrrrre.'

'Oh dear, oh dear. Milly, what *happened*?'

'I'm so sorry, I didn't mean to, I – I . . .'

'SHE DID IT ON PURPOSE!' wails Willow.

I blink back up at the empty box. *Where is she?* 'Mr Lamont, when did Mum leave? Did she see Willow fall?'

Mr Lamont's quiff shakes from side to side. 'I don't know, Milly.'

The wailing stops. 'Well, I do.' Willow's violet eyes flash in triumph. 'She saw what you did to me and died of shame. *This* time she won't forgive you, Millicent Kydd. *This* time she'll disown you FOR EVER!'

2

The Mystery of the Unapplied-for Application

Snip, snip, snip.

I grasp another chunk of hair and watch the dark clumps stick to the basin. I keep on snipping until it's the same length all over. Well, sort of.

Me and the kitchen scissors chopped off my hair the day after the Scarlet Slippers and we've been cutting it ever since. My babushka didn't say anything – she just brought me two little silver hairslides. I jab them in as she calls from downstairs.

Time for breakfast.

I sip my tea and gaze at Mum. She's dressed as the Black Swan in a beautiful black tutu, topped off with a tiara, sequins and glossy black feathers.

Eight Months On, Ballet Star Still Missing, reads the headline over the photograph in the newspaper.

Eight months on. That's two hundred and fourty-four days with no ballet. Two hundred and fourty-four nights with no Mum.

I fill up the hole in my insides with a third piece of toast.

Poor Mr Lamont. It's not his fault about the no ballet. Willow's dad said I was guilty of 'dangerous dancing'. He had 'evidence', he said. His daughter broke a fingernail *and* bruised her funny bone.

I did ask for 'evidence' of Willow Perkins's funny bone but Mr Perkins wasn't amused. I suppose it runs in the family. 'Throw her out,' he said. 'Now that her mother's gone, who's to stop you?' The other parents agreed. She's done it before. She'll do it again. So I threw myself out so Mr Lamont wouldn't have to. Goes without saying that no other ballet school would have me after that.

Across the table, Bab squints into a small gold compact. She blots her scarlet lips and pats her raven bob. This is a sign. It means I have to be quiet because she is about to call Scotland Yard. When I asked her why she wears lipstick to make a phone call, she said it made her words more 'alluring'.

Bab talks to Chief Inspector Baxter every day. Actually, most days she talks to Chief Inspector Baxter's answering machine. She says no news is good news, but to be perfectly honest, it's not good enough. I'm hoping my posters will help. Mum smiles down from every lamp post between the newsagent and the postbox. Someone somewhere must know where she is.

'Chief Inspector,' Bab purrs. 'You may as vell answer your telephone. My tango class has been cancelled and I have no plans for the rest of the day. I intend to keep leaving messages until you . . . hello? *Chief Inspector Baxter?* How vonderful to hear that manly, Glasvegian growl.'

She winks at me and pours a cup of sweet, strong coffee from the little copper coffee pot she brought with her from Moscow. Bab isn't like other people's grandmas. She doesn't knit. She doesn't bake. She doesn't nap in front of the telly and think a cup of tea is the answer to everything. But she does worry about me, I can tell. Her voice goes all chirpy.

'Is that so? If you don't mind me saying, dahhling, you are beginning to sound like an old record – no vun simply vanishes into thin air.'

I slide the newspaper under my chair so Bab won't start worrying about me again. Boris rubs his ginger furriness against my leg, then flops on top of Mum's picture. It's unusual for Boris to be so helpful. I accidentally-on-purpose drop a spoonful of boiled egg and watch him lick it all up. In the hall, the letter-box clunks and post plops onto the parquet floor. I push away my plate and get up carefully so as not to disturb him.

There's all the usual stuff. Bills, more bills, a postcard from Buenos Aires, a Christmas gift catalogue. *Free gift inside*, it says, *handy pen and torch in one*. I leave it on the hall table. Normally I'd have started looking forward to Christmas by August, but this year isn't normal.

Under a flyer for takeaway pizza is a pale-blue envelope. It's marked PRIVATE & CONFIDENTIAL. It's addressed to me.

In the kitchen, Bab huffs in Russian. Her conversation with Chief Inspector Baxter must have ended like it always does. She's still huffing when I give her the postcard.

'Bab, what's the matter?'

'Nothing, Mila.' Her Cleopatra eyes brighten. 'Ahhh, a card from Alejandro.'

I don't think I've ever had a proper letter before. I slide my finger under the flap of the envelope and pull out a typed sheet. Embossed on the pale-blue paper is a pair of black and white swans. Underneath the swans are the words, *Swan House School of Ballet*.

Little wings flutter in my ribcage.

Dear Milly,

We are super excited to inform you that your application for a scholarship to

Swan House School of Ballet has been totally successful!

Enclosed in this letter, you will find all the information you need before the new term begins. We sooo look forward to seeing you in September.

Yours truly,

Emmeline Topping, Student Liaison Person

Application? Scholarship? *Successful?*

The fluttery feeling sinks to my stomach. There must be a mistake.

Attached to the letter with a swan-shaped paperclip are three more pale-blue sheets of paper.

Term Dates and Timetables.

Uniform and Equipment.

Waiver – FOR YOUR EYES ONLY – Please read carefully and sign immediately.

A waiver? I don't remember having one of those at Mr Lamont's.

Bab props her postcard against the coffee pot. 'What have you got there, Mila?'

I stuff the waiver in my dressing-gown pocket and pass her the letter. 'It's a letter. To me. From a ballet school.'

Her coffee cup clinks on the saucer. '*Dahhling*, you've von a scholarship!'

'I KNOW! I didn't apply, did you?'

'Does it matter who applied?'

'But Bab, it must be a mistake.'

'It is not a mistake, it is *vonderful*! Let's see, you start next veek . . .' She tries not to frown at my hair. 'I suppose it vill have grown a little by then. Oh, Mila, you von't have to go back to horrid St Tilda's!'

I hadn't thought of that. A new ballet school would mean goodbye triple Science, *au revoir* scratchy jumpers, *auf Wiedersehen* grumpy teachers – which reminds me to ask Bab about her phone call with Chief Inspector Baxter say.

Bab twists the ruby on her little finger. 'The chief inspector said he vas no longer in charge of investigating your mother's disappearance.'

'Oh. Who is?'

'It's rather odd, Mila – he said he hasn't a clue.'

My hand scrunches the paper in my pocket. 'Bab, do you think they've stopped looking?'

'Of course not, dahhling.'

'Sometimes I think that she doesn't *want* to be found.'

'I've told you before, it vasn't your fault. It seems obvious to me that your mother has amnesia. It happens all the time! She is being looked after by a very nice family in Piccadilly, or thereabouts, and as soon as she remembers who she is, she vill come home. There. Now, I have kept all of your dancevear in my vardrobe. Go see if it still fits.'

Bab says this in her chirpy voice.

A chirpy Russian. It's not natural.

I give her a hug and rush upstairs.

Up in my room, I unscrunch the waiver.

Please read carefully and sign immediately.

In the case of injury, incarceration, inexplicable memory loss or death, I, the signatory, waive my right to claim against any individual, individuals or institutions employed by, or connected with, Swan House School of Ballet.

Sign Here (mandatory)..................

I speak five languages but Small Print isn't one of them. Perhaps they're being extra careful? After what happened in the Scarlet Slippers, it's a wonder I wasn't incarcerated on the spot.

At the bottom of the page there's an address.

Please return with your acceptance of our offer forthwith and absolutely as soon as possible to: Emmeline Topping,

Swan House School of Ballet, Regent's Park, London, W1.

A thought pops into my head and makes the paper tremble in my hand. If Bab didn't apply, the only other person who could have arranged the scholarship is Mum. It's MUM who's giving me the chance to dance again. Maybe if I can make up for what happened in the Scarlet Slippers, she'll come home? Maybe this is some kind of TEST?

My old ballet clothes can wait – better reply to Swan House School of Ballet before Emmeline Topping changes her mind.

After I've written my letter, I pop it in one of Bab's scented envelopes, lick the flap and tell her I'm going out. At the end of the road, a red Post Office van draws up alongside the postbox. *Forthwith*, Emmeline Topping said. *Absolutely as soon as possible.*

I start to run.

The postman jumps out of the van. He scoops the letters into his sack.

'Wait!' I thunder along the terrace and almost flatten an old man coming the other way.

'Steady on, young filly!'

It's my next door neighbour. 'Sorry, Bombardier!'

The Bombardier straightens his tweeds and smooths his whiskers. 'Oh, it's you, Milly. Just the gal I wanted to see. Remind your grandmother we have a special date tonight, what ho?'

'Will do!' Must remember to warn Bab; I expect he's going to propose again.

The postman flings the sack over his shoulder. Close up, he towers over the postbox. Either his trousers have shrunk in the wash, or they don't make post office uniforms for giants. I skid to a halt and hand him my letter. 'Lucky I caught you. This is really important. It'll be delivered by tomorrow, won't it?'

He pulls his cap over his eyes and mutters through his scarf. 'Aye, pet. I'll see to it myself.'

I'm still wondering why he was wearing a woolly scarf in August when Bab calls me upstairs. She's decided to sort through her wardrobe while I try on my things.

Bab's wardrobe is better than Narnia. It's a whole room and has sinky cream carpet and its very own Bab-like smell. Parties, perfume, mothballs – a whiff of the dry cleaners on Clapham High Street. Between her two full-length mirrors are outfits for the opera, the races, the country, the city, before ski, après ski, Moscow, Paris, Monaco . . .

She nods at Mum's old school trunk. 'Your ballet clothes are in there, Mila.'

I open the lid and pull out the stripy legwarmers Mum gave me for my birthday. Folded underneath is the girl I was eight months ago. My heart folds up too. I close the trunk quietly. How can Mum expect me to do this without her?

Bab sits me down on her chaise longue. 'Everything is much too small anyvay. Look at you, you're almost as tall as your mother now. Let's go shopping tomorrow and have lunch in Covent Garden like ve used to.'

I try on a too-small smile. 'Bab, do you think Mum would want me to dance again after what happened?'

'Of course I do, dahhling.'

'No one seemed to think so at Mr Lamont's.'

Bab huffs. 'What do they know? Vhen your mother returns, she vill find her little duckling transformed into a beautiful svan. You'll see.' She pops a gold lamé bolero over my dungarees, then tries on her Caribbean cruisewear collection. It's her way of cheering me up.

The rest of the day slips by in a blur of fake fur and sequins. I fill bags for the charity shop while Bab tells me stories about Mum – how she won her Scarlet Slipper and performed *Swan Lake* for the Queen.

As I drag the last of the bags downstairs, there's a clunk in the hall. An envelope. Pale blue. Addressed to me.

Boris follows me into the kitchen. I glance at the mantlepiece and the little scarlet *pointe* shoe perched on its golden mount.

Mum's Scarlet Slipper.

I cross my fingers. Please, *please* don't let it be a letter from Emmeline Topping saying she's made a mistake. Inside is the same embossed notepaper, but this letter isn't typed. This letter is scrawled in impatient black ink.

> Dear Milly,
> Thank you for the prompt acceptance of our offer. You will find that Swan House School of Ballet provides its students with a training like no other. I would urge you to study the enclosed prospectus carefully. It will shine a light on life at Swan House.
>
> Yours Sincerely
> Celia Sitwell, DCB
> Director

At my feet, Boris sneezes and coughs up a fur ball. My neck goes prickly. How did Celia Sitwell, DCB know I accepted her offer? I only posted my letter this morning.

When I open the prospectus, it isn't like the one at

St Tilda's. There are no smiley faces, no shiny facilities, no gushy quotes. Just lots and lots of empty pages.

Bab swoops into the kitchen. 'How odd. Ve haven't had a second post in years. Vhat does it say?'

'Nothing really. It's a prospectus from Swan House, but all the pages are empty.'

Bab flicks through it. 'The printer must be in love. I'm sure they'll send you another. Now, are you sure you don't mind if I go next door? I'll knock on the vall if the Bombardier goes down on vun knee again. Betveen the two of us, ve should be able to pull him up.'

I don't mind one bit. Bab's given up lots of things since Mum left. Cruises, Ascot, mah-jong with Mr and Mrs Ling from across the road. When I start at Swan House, she can go back to having fun again. 'You go,' I say. 'I'll make my own tea.'

She kisses my cheek. 'You are an angel. I'm so proud of you, dahhling, and Eva vould be too. I'll be home before midnight.'

Once I've tidied away Bab's clothes, I glance in the mirrors. Mum wants me to dance again, but look at me. Cutting my hair seemed like a good idea until about nine o'clock this morning. I do a little *pirouette* and *ballon* up and down a bit. I'm out of breath after three and a half minutes and my hair doesn't swish at all. How many dancers have bright-red faces, slumpy shoulders and do-it-yourself bobs? What would Mum say if she could see me now? Willow Perkins would laugh her leg warmers off.

Eight months on, and I don't even look like a ballerina.

3

The House on Swan Lake

The cab turns in to Regent's Park. We drive past a boating pond. A café. Past mums and dads taking their babies to London Zoo.

'Never been to no Swan 'ouse before,' says the cabbie. 'Is it one of them boutique 'otels?'

'Oh no,' Bab replies. 'Svan House is a school of ballet.'

'Which one of you girls is the ballerina, then?' He winks at Bab in the mirror.

Bab bats her eyelashes. 'My *daughter*. She's extremely talented.' I open my mouth and close it again.

This morning Bab gave me her favourite beret – pale blue, totally French. I'm wearing it with a stripy red-and-white top. She says if it wasn't for the dungarees, I'd look quite the *Parisien*. I suppose if I had hair like Willow Perkins I wouldn't need a beret. When Bab's hairdresser said it's still in that inbetweeny stage, he meant in between short and tragic.

'My littlest says he wants to be a ballet dancer,' says the cabbie. 'Watched that Scarlet Slipper competition on the telly. Did you see it?'

I pull my beret down over my ears.

'How charming,' says Bab in her chirpy voice. 'Have you many children?'

The cabbie chats away as the road takes us through a glade of spindly trees. In, out, in, out. The sunlight makes zebra stripes on the tarmac.

'You'd think ve vere in the countryside,' says Bab. 'Listen, Mila.'

I listen. No tooting horns. No rumbling buses. Just a soft coo-cooing coming from the treetops. On the other side of the avenue, a lake shimmers in the sunshine. A swan swoops over the water and lands on its reflection without a bump. It's like magic.

Bab points her scarlet nails at the far side of the lake. '*Ideal'no!*'

'What did you say?'

I translate for the cabbie. '*Ideal'no* – it means "perfect" in Russian.'

And it is. Swan House School of Ballet is a perfect white mansion on a perfect green lawn. The cabbie whistles. 'That must be costin' a pretty penny.'

Bab puffs up. 'Milly von a scholarship, didn't you, dahhling?'

My toes curl in my sneakers. I don't deserve a scholarship after what happened to Willow's funny bone. Mum must have pulled all kinds of strings to get me into such a smart school.

We follow the road around the lake until we reach a stone gatehouse. A hairy hand appears from the window. 'Passes please.'

Bab holds out the passes that arrived this morning.

'Thank you, Mrs Lilova,' growls a voice. 'Please proceed but make sure your driver does not leave the vehicle.'

'Fine by me, sunshine,' says the cabbie.

The hand waves us on and the wrought-iron gates creak open. Once we're through the gates, Bab reaches for her handbag and pulls out a red velvet evening bag. 'Mila, the chief inspector returned your mother's bag yesterday. I'd like you to have it.'

I try to say thank you, but the lump in my throat gets in the way.

'Open it, dahhling.'

Inside is a programme for the Sixtieth Scarlet Slipper Ballet Prize. On the cover there's a photograph of Mr Lamont and his fairies. There I am, behind Willow. Alongside *The Fairy of the Golden Vine – Millicent Kydd*, Mum's written, *Milly, age twelve*. I trace my finger over her big, loopy handwriting. There's another faint scribble next to Willow. When I tip up the programme to see what it says, a silver chain snakes into my palm.

Bab squeezes my hand. 'The chief inspector said they found Eva's charm bracelet underneath her seat.'

A shiver runs up my arm as Bab slips it over my hand and before I know it, I'm back in Mum's room – her arm around my shoulders, the bracelet heavy on my wrist. My little voice is asking, 'What are these, Mummy?'

'They're charms, Milly. They remind me of my favourite things. There's the ballet shoe Bab gave me when I won my place at the Royal Ballet School. And look, this is the little ballerina your father gave me on the day you were born.'

Dad died when I was a baby so the silver ballerina is extra special. I search the bracelet then empty Mum's bag. She's gone.

A missing ballerina. It feels like a sign. I pop the bag in my backpack and zip it up. Mustn't cry now. Not in front of Bab.

The cab ambles down a long gravel driveway. Little stones pit-pat the tyres. The front of the school comes into view and my toes curl tighter. All of the children milling around the car park have swishy hair and perfect posture.

Well. All except one.

No one seems to notice the boy puffing across the driveway like Thomas the Tank Engine. He's got headphones over his bushy, dark hair and a bushy, dark monobrow to match. An old satchel bounces across his shoulders, and there's something flapping around his neck. He's the least likely looking ballet dancer I've ever seen.

I open the cab door. Nearby, a mud-splattered car starts to reverse. As it bunny-hops backwards, three doggy faces bounce up and down in the back window. The boy and his beaten-up suitcase are in its path.

Uh-oh. He can't hear it. It can't see him. He's going to get squished.

I jump out of the cab. 'Stop!' I shout. 'STOP!'

I *grand jeté* on top of him and we thump to the ground.

Tumble, tumble. Legs. Arms. Dust. A screech in my ears. Heat on my cheeks. Smoke up my nose.

'Mila!' Bab's heels biscuit-crunch towards me. 'Mila, say something!'

I try. I try asking the boy if he's alive enough to move his sandal off my face, but it comes out as a kind of 'Fwmph.'

I give Bab a thumbs up instead.

A car door slams. A pair of dirty wellies appear

next to Bab's kitten heels. 'I'm so terribly sorry,' says a plummy voice. 'The Range Rover's a frightful mess. Been cleaning out the ponies and with the Labs in the back, I just didn't see him . . . is he hurt?'

A pair of boy's trainers skid next to the wellies. 'Looks dead to me, Mother.'

'Winded!' wheezes Thomas the Tank. 'Can't breathe.'

'Oh dear,' says the woman, 'you'd better lie still for a moment.'

The boy peers over me. I make out a halo of summery hair. An angel with a backpack for wings. I think he's laughing.

'What's so funny?'

'WHAT DID YOU SAY?' Thomas the Tank's sandal kicks my teeth. 'I CAN'T HEAR! I CAN'T HEAR!'

'It would help if you took these off,' says the angel. He pulls off the boy's headphones. 'Got a name?'

The sandal lifts off my cheek. 'It's Merv, if you must know.'

The angel pulls Merv up. 'I'm Benedict. My friends call me Sp—'

'Spencer. I know.' Merv shakes his head like he's got water in his ears, then checks the padlock on his satchel. What kind of ballet dancer has a padlock on his satchel?

I sit up. The Angel Spencer is wearing black jeans and a black leather jacket. He must be terribly hot. He pushes up his sunglasses. 'Have we met before?'

'No,' says Merv. 'Says on your number plate.' I twist my head – *SPN C5R*.

Blimey. Merv's a bit clever.

Bab takes my hand. 'Mila, dahhling, can you move your legs? Can you feel your toes?'

I pick up my beret. 'I'm fine. I can wriggle them and everything.'

'What a brave girl,' says Mrs Spencer. 'Are you all right now, Merv?'

Merv glares at me from under his eyebrow. 'Would *you* be all right if you'd been attacked by a mad Parisian?'

Possibly not that clever.

Merv makes Spencer look incredibly tall and brown. Like he's spent all summer surfing, or safari-ing, or some other outdoorsy thing beginning with 's'.

'Cheer up,' says Spencer. 'If the mad Parisian hadn't flattened you, the Range Rover would've. I'd show some gratitude if I were you.'

'Oh.'

'OK, don't overdo it.' Spencer leans against the bonnet of his car. 'As a matter of fact, she's an expert at flattening people. The hair threw me, but I never forget a face. You were that girl in the Scarlet Slippers, weren't you? Eva Kydd's daughter, right?'

'Yes, Milly. You saw it?'

Spencer has the whitest smirk I've ever seen. 'Me and the rest of the world.'

I wish he wasn't quite so loud. And tall. And brown. He's attracting way too much attention. I pull my beret over my eyes and make myself invisible.

Not really, but it worked when I was three.

Mrs Spencer carries on fussing over Merv. 'Are your parents here, Merv?' Merv shakes his head. 'Oh dear. Have you come far on your own?'

'Widecombe,' grunts Merv. 'Walked a really, really long way.'

Spencer drops the grin. 'You walked. From *Devon*?'

'No.' Merv eyes him suspiciously. 'Victoria Coach Station.'

Mrs Spencer checks her watch. 'We still have a little time – maybe I should drive you to hospital?'

Merv's monobrow shoots up in alarm. He gropes for the thing around his neck. It's a white mask like the ones people wear on the news. 'NO. WAY. Don't you know how many deadly flesh-eating bacteria there are lurking in hospitals? No way am I going to hospital.'

'Let's go,' says Spencer. 'He'll live.'

Mrs Spencer sighs. 'He really doesn't look well. What about a visit to the school nurse?'

'NO!' says Merv.

'It's the first day of term,' says Spencer. 'It'll take at least a week before zillions of flesh-eating bacteria infect the infirmary.'

Merv's eyebrow wiggles. 'Oh. OK, then.'

I fetch my backpack from the cab. Inside are my emergency supplies – a bag of mints, a term's supply of plasters and a hot-water bottle in the shape of a fat, ginger cat.

I open the mints. 'Thanks,' says Spencer, helping himself to the whole packet.

Bab smiles at him. 'You seem like a strong young man. Be a dahhling and bring Milly's trunk.'

Mrs Spencer looks surprised when her son grabs the trunk handle. She doesn't know that Bab has a mysterious way of getting people to do things. I think it has something to do with her eyelashes.

The cabbie calls after Bab, 'Don't be too long, Mrs L. Got a job waiting in Tooting.'

We all follow Merv to the steps. Either side, the white stone pillars are topped with life-size marble swans. Bab nudges Mrs Spencer. In all the excitement we hadn't noticed the enormous man at the entrance. He has two straw-coloured ponytails –

one at the back and a beardy one at the front. He is the second least likely looking ballet dancer I've ever seen.

Bab pats her bob. 'Thor in a suit and tie. I adore a vell-dressed Viking, don't you?'

Thor's ponytail beard swishes as Spencer goes past with the trunk. There's a god-like rumble. 'Where d'you think you're going? Show us your pass.'

Where have I heard that voice before?

'It's here!' Mrs Spencer waves a pass in the air. 'I'm so sorry, I did ask Ben to wear it.'

I check mine is safely around my neck.

'*Benedict Spencer*,' reads Thor. 'Put that on until I tell you to take it off.' He scowls at the rest of us. 'Go straight through the hall, past the statue, and reception's on the left. Hand in your mobiles and electrical devices at the desk.'

'No one's touching my phone,' says Spencer. 'It only came out yesterday.'

Thor squares his shoulders and the seams of his jacket sigh. 'Unauthorized devices will be destroyed. End of.'

'I've got an electric toothbrush,' I say. 'Does that count?' But Thor's already shouting at someone else.

'Gosh,' says Mrs Spencer to Bab. 'I can't see *him* in ballet tights, can you?'

'Dahhling,' sighs Bab. 'You're just not trying hard enough.'

We file into a wide, airy hall. Lots of lovely smells fill my nostrils – wood polish, lilies, fresh paint. Bab oohs and ahhs her way around the columns and arches. Caught in a beam of sunlight, a small bronze ballerina hovers *en pointe*. Spencer plonks down the trunk and I pause to read the plaque underneath.

ANNA POPOVA. FOUNDER OF THE
SCARLET SLIPPER BALLET PRIZE.
A DYNASTY IS BORN.

It's Dame Anna Popova before she was 102.

'Dame Anna has genes to die for,' says Bab. 'Every vun of her offspring has become a fabulous dancer. If you become famous vun day, they might make a statue of *your* mother.'

I wait for Spencer to make a joke, but he's too busy admiring himself in one of the huge gold mirrors.

Bab's eyes are all twinkly. 'Dahhling girl, this is your chance to make friends and start afresh. Everything vill be vonderful, I promise.' She kisses me on both cheeks and I give her a hug. As she tip-taps away, there's a tut-tut noise behind me. All of the girls in the hall are looking at me like the fairies did. Slightly suspicious and not entirely friendly. They must have seen the Scarlet Slippers too.

Even when she's not here, Willow Perkins ruins everything.

4

The Revenge of Willow Perkins

Spencer flicks a blond hair from his jacket and offers me one of my mints. 'Did you know you've ripped your trouser things and your knee's bleeding?'

I yelp at the mirror. There's a hole in my dungarees and oily black gunk all over my bottom.

'Not to worry. My father's a surgeon. I'll get him to put you on his waiting list – for a new *Kydd-knee*. See what I did there?'

'Oh, there you both are,' says Mrs Spencer. 'Now, Merv's seen the nurse, haven't you, Merv? And he's quite well, all considered. So I'll say goodbye. You will call, won't you, Ben? And remember what you said . . .'

'Yes, Mother, I'll be on my best behaviour . . .'

'Promise?'

'Promise.'

Mrs Spencer pecks him on the cheek. She doesn't notice the fingers crossed behind her son's back. She pecks me too and leans towards Merv. Merv pulls his mask over his nose.

It's not fair. Everyone else seems to have made nice, normal friends.

Mrs Spencer trots away as a gangly woman with frizzy hair and fuchsia lips approaches us. Her smile looks like it's been stuck on with sticky tape. Merv squeaks and trips over his suitcase.

'Whoopsie,' she says. Her teeth are fuchsia too. 'HONK HONK! Can I have your attention, everyone, please-thank-you.'

Spencer's still posing in the mirror. I seem to be the only one listening.

'HELLOOO, SWANLETS. There's been a teensy mistake. Suitcases should have been left in the courtyard.' She whispers to me, '*My fault*, been in bit of a flap this morning.' Then she beats her arms like a mad flamingo. 'ANYHOOO . . . who *is* this crazy lady, I hear you say.' She waffles on to no one in particular. 'My name is Emmeline Topping, but you can call me Topsy. I'm not a teacher, *obvs*, but the BRILLIANT news is – dun, dun, duh, *duhhh* – I'm going to be your MUMMY SWAN this year! Yes, swanlets, I'm going to be your housemistress – that's if I don't fail the probationary period again . . .'

Topsy's eyes go all misty. 'Dearie me. Where was I? Oh yes, before you take your suitcases outside, please can you make your way to the theatre for the director's assembly.'

Everyone starts herding down the corridor but a shriek from the galleried landing stops them in their tracks.

'MILLY, IT *IS* YOU!'

I shrink by at least two and a half centimetres. Skipping down the grand staircase is a pretty blonde girl with a white-swan neck. She's wearing a pale-blue leotard and a floaty skirt that matches her violet eyes. Her rosebud lips are all aquiver.

My heart says it can't be.

My brain says it is.

My mouth says, 'Hello, Willow.'

My legs want to run after Bab. But what if Mum knew Willow was here? What if she wants me to make amends?

What if this is THE TEST?

Garghhh.

Willow Perkins tugs off my beret. 'Millicent Kydd. What *have* you done to your hair?'

I try to snatch it back, but another girl bars my way. She's got lovely dark curls, golden eyes and a mouth that goes down in the corners.

Topsy beams. 'You two know each other? Amazeballs!' She glances at her wrist. '*Eek*, message from Ms Celia – all totally fine – be back in a tick.'

'What are *you* doing here, Millicent?' hisses Willow. 'Don't tell me you've been recruited?'

'Recruited?'

'Keep your voice down, Kydd,' says Spencer. 'POS.'

'POS?' I ask.

'He means, *Parents Over Shoulder*.' Willow nods at a couple following their daughter through the hall. The mum has tight red curls and a walk that knows where it's going. The dad has black hair and twinkling eyes just like Mr Ling's from across the road. I'm admiring the girl's swishy black hair when she turns to scowl at Willow. Her right eye is black and blue. Both are dark and fierce. Willow scowls back.

'Ouch,' says Spencer. 'Did you see her? That must have hurt.'

Willow wrinkles her nose. 'Don't waste your time feeling sorry for Li.' She reads Spencer's pass. 'I haven't seen you before.'

'First day. You?'

'I joined when Millicent lost me my Scarlet Slipper. If you want to stay out of trouble, you'll forget her and come with us.'

Spencer turns up his jacket collar. 'Actually, Trouble's my middle name. Plus, I'm famished.

Going to grab a bite in the refectory before assembly. Coming, you two?'

Merv shakes his head. 'Ah-own-oo-rwmph.'

'What did he say?' says the girl with the upside-down mouth.

Merv lifts his mask. 'I said I don't do refectories.'

'Who cares. Let's go, Bumble.' Willow rolls her eyes so far back I can only see the white bits. To be honest, I wish I could do that and still look pretty. But as Willow would say, I'd have to be pretty in the first place. She shoves my beret into my chest and storms off.

'Why didn't you go with them?' I ask Spencer.

Spencer shrugs. 'You aren't the only one who's been kicked out of their old school. We should stick together.'

'Really? What did *you* do?'

'Borrowed the headmaster's Porsche.' Spencer grins at my expression. 'I did take it back, minus the bumper. Anyway, the director got to hear about it and asked me to audition.'

'I don't believe you.'

'It's true. We Spencers are like cats. We land on our feet. Why did they ask you?'

'I have no idea. It's a bit of a mystery, really.'

'Not as much of a mystery as the contents of Merv's satchel.'

Merv backs into a breathless Topsy.

'Sorry, Merv, such a big lump. Me, not you, *obvs*. Milly, I've got to drag you away from your new besties. Someone wants to meet you.' She tugs me towards the staircase. 'Don't want to keep her waiting.'

'Who wants to meet me?'

'Just Ms Celia – *eek* – but, I'm sure it's nothing serious.'

'Do you mean Celia Sitwell, DCB? Isn't she the director?'

'Yes, but everyone calls her *Ms Celia*, as in "Mzzz". She teaches ballet and –' Topsy looks over her shoulder – 'other things. Come with me, please-thank-you – her room's in the octagon on the top floor. This way.'

I follow Topsy up the winding stairs. Why does the director of Swan House want to see me? My stomach misses a step. Maybe she's going to explain about the scholarship? Maybe she knows something about Mum?

Topsy points from the staircase. 'Keep going. This is the first floor. Wardrobe's on the right, shoes on the left.'

A snubbed pink nose appears from a small door. I watch it sniff then disappear again.

'Come along, slowcoach!' Topsy pauses on the top landing and blinks up at what looks like a smoke alarm. 'Lasers,' she says. 'Slice you in half if you don't have clearance.' Then she beams at me and I smile back.

Help. Topsy wasn't joking when she said she was crazy.

She drags me along a wide corridor and through a gallery of paintings. Portraits of ballet dancers with beautiful faces, sparkly costumes, murky backgrounds.

'Who are they?'

'This is Ms Celia's Hall of Fame. All past students. Smashtastic, aren't they? Apart from *him*, of course . . .' She shudders at a handsome boy with piercing eyes and a sly half smile. 'Those eyes follow you everywhere. Right, here we are. I'd say good luck, but that's bad luck, isn't it?'

Topsy turns a brass handle and the door creaks open. Seconds later, she's galumphing back down the stairs.

When I lean inside the octagon, it's dark. Topsy didn't say anything about it being dark.

Looks like I need more than luck; I need a handy pen and torch in one.

5
The Spy Maker

'Hello?'

I stretch my eyes wide and shuffle inside with my arms in front of me, like a mummy without the bangages.

'Open the blind so I can see you,' says a woman's voice. 'Then come nearer to the desk.'

Desk?

'*Ouch!*' Oh, *that* desk. I feel my way to the window and tug on the blind.

'Good. Can you see the laptop?'

I turn from the window and spot a computer on the desk. A woman's face flickers on screen. She gestures down a gloomy alley. 'As you can see, I'm running late, hence the video-link. I'm afraid the internet connection in this part of London is unreliable so please forgive me if we are interrupted. Do sit down, Milly.'

I plop into a comfy leather chair. 'Are you Ms Celia?'

'I am.'

I take a closer look at the face in front of me. Ms Celia's short wavy hair is a bit like mine. It's swept off her face with a green paisley scarf.

Unlike mine, her forehead is the sort that does way too much thinking.

She sizes me up with clever brown eyes. 'So, you're Eva Kydd's daughter – well, good for you—'

'Ms Celia, sorry to interrupt, but is that why I'm here? Did Mum arrange my scholarship?'

Ms Celia frowns. 'What made you think that? She had nothing to do with it.'

'So, this *wasn't* Mum's idea?' My insides sag like an old sofa. If I didn't win the scholarship, it means no more Willow. But it also means no more ballet. I don't suppose it matters. Either way, I'm going home. I push myself up. 'I understand. You made a mistake, I'd better call my babushka—'

'Sit down, Milly. You will come to know that I rarely make mistakes. Your name is Millicent Eva Catherine Kydd. Born November first, King's College Hospital, London. Weight, eight pounds, six ounces. Your mother, Eva Kydd – neé Lilova – moved from Moscow to London to study dance at the Royal Ballet School aged eleven. Your father was British and is now deceased. Your grandmother, or babushka, as you prefer to call her, is one Catherine Lilova – born in Russia to Casovan parents.' Ms Celia arches a pencilled eyebrow. 'Am I right so far?'

'H-how did you know all that?'

'You didn't read the prospectus I sent you?'

'Not exactly.'

Ms Celia sighs. 'There's one on the desk. Open it.'

The prospectus is next to the computer. I reach for it but a loud bang on screen makes me jump. Embers begin to float around Ms Celia like cherry blossom. She brushes her sleeve and squeezes between two dirty old bins.

Very odd behaviour for a grown-up, if you ask me.

She carries on as if nothing happened. 'My letter said the prospectus would shine a light on any questions you had. I would like to point out that the phrase *shine a light* was underlined. There is a second item on my desk you may find familiar.'

I pick up a Christmas gift catalogue. *Free gift inside*, it says on the cover. *Handy pen and torch in one*. 'Ooo, we got onc just like this.'

Ms Celia sighs again. 'Indeed. What do these two items have in common, I wonder? The logos, Milly, look at the logos.'

'They're both swans?'

'At last, we appear to be getting somewhere. Shine

the torch inside the prospectus.'

'But there's nothing in it.'

'Humour me – please.'

I open the cover. The moment I click the handy pen and torch in one, shapes appear on the page. There are smiley faces. Shiny facilities. And words. Lots of them.

'UV light on invisible ink,' says Ms Celia. 'Child's play. It would also have highlighted some of the more interesting subjects on the timetable we sent you.'

I gawp at the pictures. The 'facilities' include an assault course and a shooting range.

'Please turn to page five, third paragraph.'

My fingers run down the page. My eyes bulge over the words. Some are more alarming than others.

Pas de deux . . .

SURVEILLANCE . . .

Character dance . . .

CODEBREAKING . . .

Pointe work . . .

SELF-DEFENCE . . .

Yoga . . .

WEAPONS TRAINING . . .

'Blimey. Swan House, it's . . .'

'Yes?'

'It's a . . .'

'Go on.'

'It's a ballet school . . .'

'*Yes.*'

'FOR SPIES!'

Ms Celia nods. 'I knew we'd get there in the end.'

'You're not an ordinary ballet teacher, are you?'

She glances down the alley. 'Not exactly. As well as a teacher, I am an intelligence officer – agent – spy – call it what you will. You see, Milly, ballet dancers make excellent undercover agents. They are physically strong and mentally resilient. They also have good reason to travel the world.'

'You mean everyone at Swan House is going to be a spy when they grow up?'

'Those who graduate, yes. British Intelligence has a generation of Swan House dancers in their ranks. But we don't wait for you to grow up, Milly. At Swan House, we nurture the spies of the future and, when necessary, put their talents to good use. We would like you to join us.'

I blink. *Me. A spy?* 'B-but *why*?'

'You have something we need. Thanks to your grandmother, you are fluent in several languages including Casovan – *áno* or *nie*?'

'Uh, *áno*. Yes.'

'In which case, your mission is simple. We want you to befriend a young Casovan ballerina. With your ballet background and knowledge of the language, we believe you will be a perfect go-between.'

'Wh-who is she?'

'Suffice to say she's a pupil of an ex-student of ours. You will be fully briefed in good time.'

'But Ms Celia, I saw this film about spies once, and nearly all of them came to a sticky end.'

Ms Celia's lips twitch. 'I can assure you, you will receive the necessary training in spy craft to ensure you do not come to an end, sticky, or otherwise.'

'And I won't have to k-kill anyone, will I?'

'I promise you won't have to kill anyone before Christmas.'

'Is that a joke?'

No answer.

I wonder if Ms Celia is crazy too. 'I'm sorry, it really was very nice of you to ask me, but I can't accept your offer. There must be another twelve-year-old Casovan-speaking ballerina somewhere in Britain who'd make a much better spy than me.'

Ms Celia mutters under her breath. 'This has nothing to do with being *nice*, Milly. We really don't have a choice in the matter.'

'But you can't keep me here.'

'We would not choose to keep you here against your wishes, but if it came to it, we could.'

I get up. 'Bab won't let you. She'll come to get me. She won't budge until you've let me go. *Not budging* is what old ladies do best.'

'I'm afraid you're wrong, Milly. *Believing anything you tell them* is what old ladies do best. Even as we speak, your babushka is packing her bags. You will be pleased to know that we have seen to it that she has won a once-in-a-lifetime tour of Argentina. She is, and I quote, "*Obradovannaya.*"'

'Delighted?'

'Quite. You'd do well to remember that most people, young or old, believe what they want to believe.'

'But if Bab goes to Argentina, who's going to look after our cat? Boris is very picky about humans.'

'I believe your neighbour has offered to take care of him. So you see, Milly,' says Ms Celia. 'It couldn't have worked out better.'

'What if my mum comes home and no one's there?'

'I can assure you, in the eventuality that your mother returns, you will be the first to know. Now, I suggest you make your way to the theatre post haste. I have some unfinished business to attend to.'

A shout echoes down the alley behind her. Ms Celia pulls something from her jacket and backs into the shadows.

'*Wait* – please, Ms Celia, what if I can't do it? What if I'm no good at being a spy?'

'According to the Captain, you saved a boy's life today . . . I think you have—'

An explosion fills my ears. Ms Celia grimaces.

The laptop screen goes black.

6

Cycni Venustas, Cor Leonis

'Have what?' I shout at the laptop. '*Have what?*'

No Mum?

No Bab?

No clue what's going on?

Suddenly there are two bendy straws where my legs used to be.

I wobble towards Ms Celia's gallery, and pause to let my knees catch up. Underneath the portrait of the man with the shifty eyeballs is an inscription.

Ivan Korolev in his role as Von Rothbart, Swan Lake.

Swan Lake. The ballet that made Mum famous.

I take a closer look at the painting. A winged cape hangs around the boy's shoulders. Black feathers gleam green and gold against his skin. A tiny glass bottle glints in his hand. It's etched with a skull and crossbones.

No wonder he gives Topsy the jitters.

I move along the line of paintings. Strapped to the tights of a girl in a lilac tutu is a dagger. The skinny little boy next to her is karate chopping the air. I read the name under the painting. *Filipp Popov*.

'What are you gawpin' at?' I turn and recognize the girl with the black eye. She bounds down the corridor and pulls up an inch from my nose.

'One of the *Popovs* was a spy?'

'Yeah. So?'

'It's hard to take in, that's all. Until a few minutes ago, I thought this was an ordinary ballet school.'

The girl tucks a folder under her arm and I notice a scrape along her knuckles. 'No one told you this is a spy school? But I just saw you talkin' to Princess Perkins downstairs.'

'Willow Perkins wouldn't tell *me* anything.'

'You ain't a friend of hers then?'

'Not exactly. You?'

'I'd rarver be friends wiv a rattle snake – at least you can hear them comin'.' The girl holds out her hand. 'Name's Lottie. Lottie Li. What's your name?'

'You don't recognize me from the Scarlet Slippers?'

'Nah, between you an' me, ballet ain't really my fing.' Lottie's smile comes with dimples and a gap in her front teeth.

'I'm Milly. Milly Kydd.' I smile back and point at

the painting behind me. 'He doesn't look like a Popov. What happened?'

'Dunno – before my time. All I know is his family's famous, but he never came to much. Anyway, you'd better get goin'. Assembly's about to start and Madame's a stickler for timekeepin'.' Lottie nods at her folder. 'I'll catch you up. Got to leave my translations on Ms Celia's desk. She's old school. Likes hard copies of everyfink.'

'Translations?'

'Just a bit of Mandarin and Malay – my dad's side's from Singapore. Tryin' to learn Russian too but even the names do my head in.'

'My mum's half Russian. I could help, if you like.'

Lottie backs towards the octagon. 'I might take you up on that! My mum's from Hackney – her only language is Cockney. Fat lot a good that is in Vladivostock. Is your dad Russian too?'

I feel for the ballerina on Mum's bracelet but she's gone. 'No, he's English, but he died when I was a little.'

'Sorry,' says Lottie. 'Me and my big mouf.'

'It's all right,' I say in Bab's chirpy voice. 'It was a long time ago and I never really knew him. Anyway, I'd better go. Do you know where the theatre is?'

'Turn left at the bottom of the stairs, cross the hall then take the door on the right. Carry on straight fru' the double doors and Bob's your aunty. Save me a seat!'

I rush down the stairs. Left at the bottom. Across the hall.

Which door? I search for someone to ask but the hall is all air and echoes.

A hand pats my back. 'I thought you might like company,' says Willow Perkins. 'Walking into a room with everyone staring and talking about you must be cringy.' She pulls a sad face. 'But you'd know that better than anyone.'

'Uhh, thanks, Willow.' Why is she being so nice all of a sudden?

Her eyelids flutter. 'Listen, Milly. I know we haven't always been the best of friends, but I'd like to put everything behind us and start again.'

'You would?'

'Absolutely. What do you say?'

Lottie saves me from answering. 'She bovverin' you, Milly?

'Run along, Li,' says Willow. 'This is a private conversation.'

Lottie juts out her dimply chin. 'Why don't you run along, Perkins, before I smack this over your kale 'ole.'

I don't think Lottie realizes she only comes up to Willow's armpits. She peels something off my back. It's a piece of paper with one word in big, red letters.

BACKSTABBER.

Willow's eyes darken. 'I'd watch yourself if I were you, Li. When Milly falls, she drags her friends down with her.' Then for no reason at all, she starts to sob. Lottie spins around as footsteps pad along the corridor.

A twig-thin woman with long, white hair swoops towards us. A white skirt swishes at her ankles. A white scarf shimmers at her throat. Judging by her frosty expression, Willow Perkins is in serious trouble.

'Willow?' says the woman. 'Is there a problem, *ma chère*?'

Willow sniffs. 'They were trying to make me wear *that*, Madame.'

The woman snatches the sign from Lottie. 'What is zis?'

Lottie clenches her fists. 'She's lyin'!'

'Willow, you may go.'

'Yes, Madame. Thank you, Madame.' Willow bolts through the doors.

Madame's grey eyes ice over. 'Have I not warned you before, Charlotte Li? It is not even twelve o'clock and already you are making trouble. Look at you! What did you do to your eye – and your hand also? Always it is ze fisticuffs!'

Lottie shrugs. 'No one bullies a friend of mine and gets away wiv it. And I did like the Captain said, I never broke no rules – only used my fists.'

Madame tuts. '*Only used your fists?*' She frowns at my dungarees and tuts again. 'And *you*. What have you got to say for yourself? It is your first day, yes?'

'Yes, but it wasn't Lottie's fault just now—'

'*Enough*. Another incident like zis and it will be your last. And take off your hat when you address me.' I tug off my beret and my bracelet jangles.

Madame's eyes widen. 'If you had read our prospectus you would know zat Swan House does not allow jewellery. Give zat to me.'

I slip off the bracelet and clutch it behind my back. 'But, Madame, it's my mum's. I won't wear it again, I promise.'

'Give it to me, I said.'

I can't help it. I do a little stomp. 'No.'

Madame lifts my chin with a long, white fingernail. 'No one says *non* to Madame.' She grabs my wrist and seizes Mum's bracelet. 'Charlotte, you will see me after supper. *Millicent Kydd* – you should choose *tes amis* more carefully.'

Madame marches into the theatre and the doors swing in our faces.

Lottie groans. 'I keep forgettin' I promised Ms Celia I'd count to a hundred when I got angry.'

My wrist is red where Mum's bracelet should be. 'Is she always so horrible?'

'Yeah, Madame is as bad as Perkins. Did I tell you she got my room-mates turfed out last term?'

'Really?' I trail Lottie into the theatre and Madame pops out of my head. I gawp at the golden balconies, the velvety curtains, the swans painted on the sky-blue ceiling. The back of the stage is open to the lake. Branches sway in the breeze. Real life swans glide on the sparkling water. It's small and utterly *ideal'no*.

'Wow.'

Lottie shrugs. 'S'all right, ain't it. C'mon, there are three empty seats near the boy wiv the . . . wait a minute, is he wearin' a *mask*?'

We squeeze between lots of boney knees and squash either side of Merv. Spencer's slouched in the chair in front.

'Is the back of the stage always open?' I ask.

'Only when it's sunny,' replies Lottie. 'It's a right lark – you can dive into the lake from up there.'

Merv pulls down his mask. 'Only if you want to get expelled. Anyway, the shutters are closed most of the time for security purposes.'

'Who asked you?' says Lottie.

'This is Merv,' I say. 'Merv, this is Lottie Li.'

Lottie pulls a face. 'What's wiv the mask?'

Merv blinks. 'It's for protection.'

'Protection against what?'

'Pollution, dust, bacteria, viruses—'

'Wish I'd never asked,' says Lottie.

I point at a glass box suspended above the exit behind us. 'What's that, Lottie?'

'It's the control room, where they keep all the sound and lightin' and stuff.'

I think Merv's grunt is Mervish for 'Awesome'.

Spencer twists around in his chair and stares at Lottie.

Lottie glares back. 'What are you lookin' at? Ain't you seen a black eye before?'

'OK, Shorty. Keep your tights on.'

'Who are you callin' short?' Lottie jumps up. 'You want to go outside?'

Spencer pulls a please-don't-hurt-me face, then laughs. 'I should warn you – I'm a blue-belt in tae-kwondo.'

'Ooooo,' says Lottie. 'I'm so scared. NOT.' Luckily, Madame claps for silence and a hush falls like snow.

'Welcome to Swan House School of Ballet. My name is Madame de La Cloche, your Head of Ballet. I have one short announcement to make before ze director makes her speech, and it is zis: ze term ahead, it will be dark, it will be dangerous. You might think it is warm outside, but for every one of you, ze summer is now *over*.'

Merv squeezes his satchel. Lottie kicks Spencer's chair. Spencer slips his sunglasses into his pocket. Outside, there's a rumble which sounds like thunder, but as it draws nearer, Lottie whispers in my ear. 'That'll be Ms Celia and Winifred.'

'Who's Winifred?'

'You'll see,' says Lottie.

Behind Madame, a pair of steel shutters grate together and I watch *ze summer* disappear. A large screen lowers in front of the shutters and Ms Celia strides out from the wings. There's a rip in her trousers and a black smudge on her cheek. Her smile is so brief, I wonder if I imagined it.

'Thank you, Madame,' she says in a no-nonsense voice. 'I will follow your example and get straight to the point.

'As most of you know, every year, the Popov family invite three schools to compete in the Scarlet Slipper Ballet Prize. This year is no exception, and this morning the selected schools were announced.'

She gestures behind her and photographs of two men light up the screen. A chubby one hugging a trophy and a scary one in a black fur coat.

'The gentleman on my right, holding the trophy for Texan Ballet School of the Year is Dick Van Twinkle – director of Van Twinkle's Stars of Tomorrow. On my left, and making a return to the world of ballet, is Ivan Korolev, founder of the leading ballet school in Casova, the Korolev Dance Academy.'

The girl next to Spencer gasps.

Ivan Korolev? Wasn't he the boy in the painting – the one with the bottle of poison?

Ms Celia turns to face us. 'You will be pleased to learn that the third and final school to take part in the Scarlet Slippers this year, and hosting the competition, is Swan House School of Ballet.'

The Scarlet Slippers? At Swan House?

My hand flies to my throat. I feel like I'm about to cough up a furball.

Ms Celia holds up her hand for silence. 'Girls and boys, we are not entering on a whim. We are entering because we have a mission . . .'

Spencer straightens to attention. Lottie punches the air. Merv almost falls off his chair.

Ms Celia begins to pace. 'The Scarlet Slippers provide an opportunity to lure our old friend Ivan Korolev to London. Some of you may be alarmed at the name, and so you should be. Korolev was once a student at Swan House and now controls the only other school in the world to mirror our own. But where we seek to uphold harmony and peace, Korolev incites discord and war. He is a dangerous adversary.'

I whisper to Merv, 'What about the Stars of

Tomorrow? Are they spies too?'

'If you'd been listening, you'd have heard Ms Celia say that Swan House and Korolev's Academy are the only two schools—'

'SHHH,' says the girl next to Spencer.

Ms Celia stops pacing and her forehead wrinkles in my direction. 'I have done what I can to secure our place in the competition. But now it is up to you. It is *vital* that Swan House excels or suspicions will be aroused. If we fail, lives may be lost. That is all you need to know for now. You have less than four months of training before we host the competition. *Cycni venustas . . .*'

A chorus of voices join in, ' . . . *COR LEONIS!*'

Ms Celia thrusts her hands in her trouser pockets and steps back into the shadows. The faces disappear from the screen and up pops the school badge. The pair of swans morph into a lion's head and a roar rattles the theatre. When the lion fades away, all that's left is the school motto.

Cycni venustas, cor leonis.

'Grace of a swan, heart of a lion,' says Spencer.

'Know a bit of Latin, do you?' says Lottie. 'Ain't you Mr La-di-da.'

'There's nothing wrong with being smart.'

'What's smart about speakin' some old language no one uses no more?'

Spencer grins. 'I couldn't agree more. Who needs to speak Latin when you have a phone in your pocket?'

'A phone?' splutters Merv. 'You were supposed to hand in your electrical devices at reception!'

'So? Do you always do what you're told, Merv?'

'Can't answer that without my lawyer present,' says Merv.

Lottie scowls. 'Smugglin' stuff into Swan House ain't smart. You'll be laughin' on the other side of your face when you're doin' the Dance of Deaf.'

I don't get to find out what the Dance of Deaf is, because Madame is back onstage. With a click of her long white fingers, the screen rises, the shutters grind apart and the lake reappears.

'*Mes enfants*. Before ze Captain makes his presentation, I have one last thing to say. Some of you may think your karate kicks are more important than your *chaînés* turns. *Think again*. To dance in ze Scarlet Slippers is to dance as you have never danced before.'

Lottie nudges Merv. 'My *chaînés* are rubbish. I'm guessin' yours ain't too clever neiver. Where did you train?'

'Nowhere.'

'So, who taught you?'

'No one.'

'You taught *yourself* to dance?'

'I don't dance.'

'But we all got to dance.'

'Not me,' says Merv. 'I'm special.'

At that moment, the stage doors crash open and Thor marches down the aisle. His ponytail swishes one way, his beard swishes the other.

'The Captain's a legend,' whispers Lottie. 'Tough as old boots, he is. Take a butcher's at his fingernails. All missin'.'

My chair trembles. Or maybe it's my knees.

'Thank you, Madame,' booms the Captain. 'This won't take long . . .'

Turns out Thor's mortal name is Captain Thurgood and his home on Earth is Newcastle upon Tyne. He folds his Viking arms. 'Now that the intro's over, everyone can look under their seats.'

I grope under my chair and find a pale-blue kit bag. The theatre fills with the sound of zips unzipping. We all pull out identical slim wallets.

The Captain climbs the steps up to the stage and draws something from his wallet. 'This is everything you need for now. It's the latest Swanphone and as you can see, it's no ordinary phone. It's one of the smartest devices on the planet. Turn it on and you'll get the idea.'

Blimey. My first ever smartphone and it's the

smartest device on the planet!

Spencer tosses his old phone into his bag.

The Swanphone weighs less than a feather. It's slimmer than an ordinary phone and totally see-through.

I whisper to Merv, 'I can't find the buttons. How do you switch it on?'

'You talk to it,' says Merv, like he can't believe I've never seen a Swanphone before.

'Hello, there,' I say, like I've got ten at home. 'How are you today?'

My Swanphone glows. 'Hello, Millicent Kydd, I am charged and ready to go, thank you for asking.'

Lottie sticks her nose in the air. 'Posh, ain't it. Sounds just like *him*.'

Luckily, Spencer's too glued to his Swanphone to hear.

I'm still confused. 'How it does it know who I am?'

'It recognizes your DNA.' Merv says this *verrry* slowly. 'You do know what genes are?'

'Of course I do. But how can it recognize my genes? I've only been here for three hours.'

'Saliva,' says my Swanphone.

'Uh?'

Merv grunts. 'Your reply letter? You licked the envelope?'

Blimey.

'Your Swanphone is made of smart silicone,' says

the Captain. 'It appears to be transparent because it possesses a chameleon-like ability to mirror its environment. It's also extremely flexible. See . . .' He holds up his Swanphone and bends it around his wrist like a bangle. The phone disappears. 'As good as invisible.' He holds the phone under Willow Perkins's nose and a ripple of applause runs across her row.

I wrap my phone around my wrist.

Wow.

'The Swanphone does everything you'd expect from a smartphone and more. As well as planning your school day, it tracks where you go. It monitors your health. It has environmental and weather sensors. It also has an inbuilt weapons system which you'll be able to access once you've completed your training.'

'Yes!' says Spencer.

'So, now to your mentors. Existing students, you'll be happy to know your mentors have been transferred to your upgraded Swanphones. If you're new to Swan House, stand up for the Pairing.'

The Pairing?

I look around as a handful of people shuffle to their feet. Spencer gestures at Merv. 'You heard the Captain – stand up.'

Merv folds his arms. 'Technically, I'm not new.'

'You too, Merv,' booms the Captain.

'Go for it, Milly,' says Lottie. 'This is the fun bit.'

I stand up. With any luck, the Captain can't see me behind Spencer.

'No point in hiding behind Spencer, Kydd,' says the Captain. 'You're first up. Ask it nicely and your Swanphone will activate your virtual mentor.'

I do as I'm told and my wrist glows.

'We know you lot pay more attention to your peers than us,' says the Captain, 'which is why we ask all of our students to sign up to the mentor program before they graduate. We then create avatars that are programmed to help with your personal development and act as guides and advisors from now until you leave.'

Avatars? I whisper to Merv, 'What's the mentor programme?'

Merv grunts. 'That's MNTR. Your data was fed into the program when you accepted your place. It assessed your background, personality type, strengths and weaknesses, then paired you with one of the alumni on its database.'

I have no idea what he's talking about.

Merv points at the empty chair next to me. 'I mean him.'

I double take.

There's a boy on the chair . . .

And I can see right through him.

'Kydd,' says the Captain. 'Say hello to Filipp Popov.'

Filipp Popov has see-through mousey hair, see-through mousey ears and see-through mousey teeth. His see-through mousey hands are shaking. He looks like he needs a hug.

My new mentor is the third least likely looking ballet dancer I've ever seen.

7

The Heart Maker

Filipp Popov shakes his mousey head. 'Please wait while I reboot. There appears to be a malfunction.' His words whistle through his teeth.

'There hasn't been a malfunction, Popov. You've been paired with Milly Kydd.'

Filipp Popov puffs out his bony chest and I realize he's not shaking with nerves, he's shaking with rage. 'In that case, I wish to make a formal complaint. When I signed up to offer my services as a mentor – I did not expect to be paired with someone like *her*.'

Does he mean me?

The Captain strokes his ponytail beard. 'It's nowt to do with us, Popov. Blame the program.'

'Then there must be a fault with the program.'

'No,' mutters Merv. 'The MNTR program is never wrong! NEVER!'

Filipp Popov waves a boney wrist at Merv. 'Who's *he*?'

The Captain pulls a book from his pocket. '*He's* the new programmer. Rule One of *The Guide to Espionage*. Never judge a book by its cover.'

Filipp Popov's cheeks turn as red as a Scarlet Slipper. 'But doesn't he know who I am? Without my grandm-mother, there would be no Scarlet Slipper! And *she* –' he definitely means me – 'almost turned the competition into a laughing stock!'

Laughter fills the theatre. It's not easy to look dignified with a pink face and oily bottom, but I try my best.

'How does Filipp Popov know so much about me?' I whisper to Merv.

'Because the mentors are constantly updated with information about their students.'

'Quiet you lot,' barks the Captain. 'Sorry, Popov – you're stuck with each other. Kydd, the good news is you can turn him off whenever you like.'

The Captain checks his Swanphone. 'I'll say this for you, Merv, that program of yours has got Popov's personality down to a T. Now, can we get on with it? Who's next? *Philpot*, where are you?'

Filipp Popov's angry little face vanishes into thin air and I wish I could vanish too, but I have to endure the rest of the Captain's presentation with everyone staring and talking about me. 'Cringy' doesn't come close.

'OK, Merv. Your turn,' says the Captain.

Merv mutters into his Swanphone and a human-shaped tornado somersaults over my head and lands at Merv's feet.

Lottie claps as the boy bows to Merv. 'Greetings, Merv. I am Han Wu. It is an honour to be paired with you.'

Spencer grins at Merv's shocked expression. 'Like you said, Merv, the software's never wrong.'

'OK, Spencer,' booms the Captain. 'You're last up – you know what to do . . .'

Seconds later, a flickering, dark figure appears in the aisle. The girl closest to it screams and people stand up to get a better look. The Captain rumbles, 'Sit down, everyone. It's only a bliddy hologram.'

The boy runs a hand through his bluebottle-black hair. He smiles a half smile at Spencer.

'Spencer,' says the Captain. 'Meet Ivan Korolev.'

Spencer gives Merv a look of desperation. 'But Ms Celia said he was the bad guy.'

'This isn't the Korolev we all know and love,' says the Captain. 'Your mentor is the young Ivan. Isn't that right, Merv?'

Merv hrumphs.

'How old are you, Ivan?' asks the Captain.

'Fifteen,' says the virtual Ivan Korolev.

'Hear that, Spencer? At fifteen, Ivan was a promising dancer and a budding young spy. But the important thing is, he was still on our side, weren't you, son?'

'Of course,' says the boy. 'I am on the side of harmony and peace.'

'As are we all,' says the Captain. 'Spencer, you can ask your programmer friend why you've been paired with Ivan later. We've got to get a move on. I'm starving.'

'Thank you, Captain,' says Madame. 'But before zey have lunch, ze children must collect zeir uniforms from Mademoiselle Topping.'

I trudge through the hall after Merv and Lottie and wonder what would happen if I just kept going. Willow Perkins catches my eye and elbows the boy next to her. He barges into me.

'*Oi*, Debello.' Lottie grabs his sleeve. 'Mess wiv Milly and you mess wiv me, got it?'

The boy sticks up his hands. 'Sorry, Li. I didn't know she was with you.'

'Well, you know now.' When Lottie links her arm through mine, my insides glow like a Swanphone.

We join a long queue of students waiting for their

uniforms. I keep walking through virtual people. It's very discombobulating, as Bab would say.

Merv sidles away but Lottie nabs his collar. 'How come you've got the second coolest mentor in school?'

Merv wriggles out of her grasp. 'Like I said, the program assesses our strengths *and* weaknesses. For some reason, it must think I need Han Wu to help me with self-defence.'

'Nah, really?' Lottie digs me in the ribs.

'If Han Wu is the second coolest mentor in school, who's the first?' I ask, rubbing my side.

Lottie's cheeks dimple. 'I'll show you. Yo, Nora!'

A shimmering girl appears in front of us. Her tutu is scattered with lilacs and velvety leaves. Her hair is woven with petals. She's the loveliest Lilac Fairy I've ever seen.

'Everyone, this is Nora Doone.'

Nora Doone smiles. 'Welcome back, Lottie. How can I help you?'

'Can you dance for my friend, Milly?'

'Of course.' Nora *pirouettes* and the air seems to sigh.

Lottie doesn't even look up from her Swanphone. 'Fanks, Nora. You can go now.'

Nora Doone curtsies and a wisp of honey hair escapes her bun. I sigh too. 'I could have watched her for ever.'

Lottie chews her lip. 'Yeah, she's a proper legend. Died in action the year I was born.'

I bump back to earth. Madame said the year ahead was going to be dark and dangerous. We're not here to just dance.

Lottie scowls as a tall blond boy barges in front of us.

'Hey, Merv,' says Spencer, 'what do you think you're doing pairing me with *Korolev*?'

'*I* didn't pair you with anyone,' says Merv. 'The *program* did. Probably because you were both kicked out of school. I seem to remember you saying that Trouble was your middle name.'

'I didn't think of that,' says Spencer. He slaps Merv on the back and Merv starts to splutter. 'So, Merv, you don't dance. You don't fight. What exactly do you do?'

Merv looks shifty, or maybe he's smiling, it's hard to tell. 'I'm in charge of IT and cybersecurity.'

Spencer folds his arms. 'You're *twelve*. How can you be in charge of cyber-anything?'

'I've been working for MI5 since I was eight.'

'Oh yeah. What did you do at MI5?'

'Can't talk about that, but at Swan House I oversee all the tech, plus the hidden cameras, microphones . . . can't talk about the rest.'

'There are hidden cameras?' I say. 'In the school?'

'That ain't nuffink new,' says Lottie. 'Swan House has always had secrets. The house was built by some spy—'

'Lord Astus,' says Merv.

'That's the one. Cos some old king—'

'George the Third,' says Merv.

'That's him. Gave him the land as a fank you for foilin' an assassination attempt.'

Merv shuffles up the queue. 'That's why Swan House ended up being a school. In his will, Lord Astus decreed it had to remain in the service of British Intelligence. So, when it was eventually inherited by a dancer, she had the idea to combine ballet with espionage.'

Spencer yawns. 'That's all fascinating, but why's Crazy Lady taking so long? I'm famished.'

'It's Perkins's fault,' says Lottic. 'There's somefink wrong wiv her new uniform.'

Willow is at the front of the queue, moaning at Topsy. 'This is *much* too big,' she snuffles. 'I need a smaller one.'

'I'm ever so sorry, Willow. But there aren't any more. We're waiting for the next delivery of extra-stretchy lycra.'

The snuffle turns into a sob. 'I really don't want to make trouble, Topsy, but if you can't find me another leotard, I'll just have to complain to Madame.'

Topsy grabs her arm. 'No! I mean, please, Willow.

I'll try to find you one. Just please don't say anything to Madame. I'm on probation, you see . . .'

Willow dabs her eyes. 'Thank you so much. Have it sent to my dorm, would you?' She and Bumble giggle as they head to the refectory.

'Don't know how she gets away wiv it,' says Lottie. 'She tried blackmailin' me once. Soon stopped when I showed her why I'd been recruited.'

'Why were you recruited?' asks Spencer.

'Cos of this.' Lottie grabs Merv's head in an armlock.

'Gerroffme!' yelps Merv.

'Black belt in kung fu,' pants Lottie. 'More fun than flamin' ballet, I can tell you.'

'Do you think you'd better let go of him now?' I say.

'Oh, yeah, sorry, Merv. No harm done.'

Merv clutches his throat and starts to croak, 'Han Wuuuu.'

'Glad she's on my side,' says Spencer.

Lottie's dimples vanish. 'Who said I'm on your side?'

I almost jump out of my dungarees when Han Wu leaps right through her. 'How can I serve you, Merv?'

'Keep her away from me,' wheezes Merv.

Han Wu bows. 'As you wish. Would you like me to apply my Snake Hand or my Tiger Claw?'

Lottie is already jabbing her fists. 'Come on then, Wu, let's see what you got.'

Merv yelps. 'I don't want you to *fight* her.'

'Spoilsport,' says Lottie. 'I'm itchin' to practise my Tiger Claw.'

Han Wu frowns. 'Itching? Does Little Li have a rash? I highly recommend Tiger Balm for most—'

Han Wu vanishes and Merv groans. 'I think I've created a monster.'

Merv is still wheezing when we reach the front of the queue. 'Ooo, I've been looking for you three!' says Topsy. 'You've got fittings at Meekes the Shoemaker's in half an hour. Not you, Merv – you're special.'

My stomach twirls. Meekes used to be my favourite shop in the world.

'But I'm still growing. I need food,' says Spencer. 'Can't you change the appointment?'

'Sorry, swanlets – no time. Ms Celia's going to take you to Covent Garden.You'll find her in the coach house.'

'The coach house?'

'It's where the lords and ladies kept their carriages in the olden days. You know, when stables had horses snoozing in them, not children. Things have changed a bit since then.' Topsy glances at her wrist. 'She should be on her—'

'Emmeline,' says a no-nonsense voice behind us. 'You have lipstick on your teeth.'

Ms Celia has scrubbed her face and changed into another pair of trousers. She's wearing what Bab would describe as gentlemen's shoes. 'Chop chop, Emmeline. Our appointment is at one.'

'Nearly almost done, Ms Celia.'

'I imagine you've been to Meekes before, Milly?'

'Oh yes,' says Topsy, 'Milly must have—'

'Let the girl speak for herself, Emmeline.'

I pull back my shoulders. Ms Celia has the kind of gaze that makes you stand up straighter. 'I used to go with my mum. She had all her shoes made at Meekes.'

I don't mention that Willow always came too.

'Naturally – Meekes employs the best shoemakers in the world. We wouldn't buy our shoes from anywhere else. Emmeline, you have *five* minutes.' We watch people make way as she strides down the corridor.

Topsy rubs her teeth with a stubby finger. 'Isn't she awesome? You'd better run. Lottie will show you where to go, won't you, Lottie, please-thank-you.'

'What about our kit?' says Spencer.

'Oh, yes. Silly me. Such a birdbrain.' Topsy hands out our uniforms and ballet kit. Hoodies, T-shirts, tights and leotards – all embroidered with the school badge.

'Honk. Honk. See you later, swanlets!'

Spencer and I follow Lottie past the staircase. 'Quickest way's fru the door to the lake,' she says.

We follow her into a large, sunny courtyard. Lottie points at the long red-brick building ahead. Either side of an archway dripping with wisteria are two gleaming garage doors.

Ms Celia is busy loading the boot of her car. It's the colour of strawberries and cream and makes me think of picnics and The Famous Five. Someone with blonde hair is already in the front seat.

'Put your uniforms in the boot then jump in the back,' says Ms Celia. 'There's plenty of room.'

'Didn't know *she* was comin',' says Lottie.

Ms Celia climbs in. 'Willow has an order to collect from Meekes. What are you waiting for, Benedict?'

Spencer is hovering near the bonnet of Ms Celia's old car. 'Topsy mentioned horses. I think we'll need them if we want to get to Covent Garden before Christmas.'

'Finks he's a right joker, don't he?' says Lottie.

'Young man,' replies Ms Celia, 'I can assure you that Winifred goes all by herself. For your information, she's a Morris Minor 1000 Traveller and a classic to boot. She's never let me down, which is more than I can say for most people.'

'Thought this was spy school,' says Spencer. 'Can't

see *Winifred* in a high-speed car chase, that's all I'm saying.'

'Rule Two of *The Guide to Espionage*,' says Ms Celia. 'Never judge a car by its bonnet.'

Spencer ducks in next to Lottie and snaps at Willow, 'Hey, Perkins, move your seat forward.'

Willow turns to glare at him. 'There's no need to take it out on me.'

'Take what out on you?'

'Being paired with a traitor.'

'I presume you're talking about Ivan,' says Ms Celia. 'Benedict is lucky – the last child Ivan mentored did very well. Now, belt up, everyone!'

'Yeah,' says Lottie. 'Belt up, Perkins.'

When Topsy said Ms Celia taught 'other things', turns out driving is one of them – cars, motorbikes, helicopters, aeroplanes. By the time we arrive in Covent Garden, Willow is green and Lottie is hoarse from whooping around the corners. I'm glad I gave my breakfast to Boris this morning.

Ms Celia screeches alongside the pavement and reverses into a tiny space.

'You can't park here,' says Spencer. 'They'll tow your car.'

Ms Celia raises an eyebrow. 'I'd like to see them try.'

She leads us into a cobbled street tucked between Soho and Covent Garden.

The moment I see Meekes's shiny red door, the memories tiptoe back. We're greeted by the tinkle of a bell and a waft of leather, glue and the perfume of a lady with enormous arms and tiny wrists.

'Good afternoon, Ms Celia. Are these my two thirty fittings?'

'They are, Mrs Huntley-Palmer. We'll take three pairs of flats each and the girls also need *pointe* shoes. Did Emmeline tell you we'll need them all for tomorrow?'

Mrs Huntley-Palmer tuts. 'No, she did not. But for you, Ms Celia, we will attempt the impossible.'

Mrs Huntley-Palmer ushers us through the shop at the front of the building. Everything is just as I remember – the whirly carpet, the old-fashioned till, the rows of pink satin ballet shoes.

'I ain't been here before,' says Lottie.

'That's because you're not ready for handmade shoes,' says Willow.

'What are you tryin' to say, Perkins? That I ain't good enough?'

'Lottie, remember what I said about self-control,' warns Ms Celia. 'It was my decision to bring Lottie, Willow. We have a very important "competition" and we need students with Lottie's skills to be part of it. I've promised Madame that you will work harder at your dancing this term, Lottie. Don't let me down.'

'Fanks, Ms Celia. I will try, honest.'

'Now if you don't mind, Mrs Huntley-Palmer, I'll leave the children with you. Wait here until I return, everyone, and do *not*, under any circumstances, leave the premises. That applies to all of you,' she adds, staring at Spencer.

When Ms Celia has left, Willow Perkins pushes her way to the front. 'Mrs Huntley-Palmer, I don't need a fitting. I'm here to collect an order.'

'Your maker?'

'Heart Maker.'

'Wait here, Miss Perkins. I'll be with the rest of you in a moment.'

'Does Heart Maker still work here?' I ask Mrs Huntley-Palmer.

'He does indeed. Goodness me, it's Milly Kydd, isn't it? Go on down, Milly – he'll be delighted to see you again.'

The drone of sewing machines gets louder as Spencer and Lottie follow me down a rickety staircase. In the basement, a handful of men in aprons crouch over their benches. We watch as they scrape, hammer, cut and shape small scraps of satin into ballet shoes. I remember Mum saying her shoemaker's hands were as misshapen as her feet.

'Well, I never! Is that you, Miss Millicent?'

'Mr Stubbs!'

Mr Stubbs wipes his bent old hands on his apron before cupping them around mine. His shaggy eyebrows are speckled with sawdust.

'I knew you'd be back – once a ballerina, always a ballerina, I say. It's like me Uncle Bob at Meekes – gets in the blood. Still no news of your mum, miss? I think about 'er every time I make a pair of size fours.'

My eyes sting as the tiptoeing of memories turns into a stampede.

'Aw, sorry, miss – I shouldn't 'ave said nothin'. She's a lovely lady, your mum – not many of 'em take the time to come down 'ere and talk to us makers. If you don't mind me sayin', you've turned into the spit of 'er.' He peers at my feet. 'Size fours too now. You've 'ad a bit of a spurt.'

'I have a bit. How are you, Mr Stubbs?'

'Tickety-boo, miss. Tickety-boo.' He points at the nook under the stairs. 'You won't 'ave met me new apprentice. Come over an' say 'ello to Miss Millicent, Pip. She's Eva Kydd's daughter.'

Mr Stubbs's apprentice glances up from under his fringe. His face is speckled with freckles.

'Young Pip's a natural. What are you now, Pip?

Eighteen? Nineteen? If you keep up the 'ard work, you'll be stepping into my shoes one day.'

Pip blushes to his gingery roots. 'If I get to be half as good as you, I'll be happy.' He smiles at me. 'Heart Maker's a legend. He's the only shoemaker Dame Anna trusts to make the Scarlet Slipper trophy. Isn't that right, Heart Maker?'

Mr Stubbs beams. 'True enough. Miss Millicent 'as one of 'er mum's at 'ome.'

'I'm a big fan, miss,' says Pip. 'I saw her dance *Swan Lake* on the telly once.' He blushes again. 'I've never forgotten it.'

I give Mr Stubbs's apprentice the smile I keep for grown-ups I like.

'Why do they call you Heart Maker?' Lottie asks.

'And who's this young lady? I never forgets a pair o' plates but I'm not so good at faces.'

'This is Lottie,' I explain, 'she hasn't had a pair of shoes made for her before.'

Mr Stubbs scratches his nose. 'Well, it's like this, Miss Lottie – we makers stamp a mark on the soles of every shoe we craft. See Scarpelli over there – 'is mark is a star, so we call 'im Star Maker. Young Bert's is a diamond – so 'e's Diamond Maker. And mine's an 'eart, so . . .'

'You're Heart Maker, I get it,' says Lottie.

'You can take a butcher's at a pair I just finished,

if you like.'

Mr Stubbs leads us to his bench and hands Lottie a *pointe* shoe. 'It's for one of your lot. She's a bit hoity-toity, if you know what I mean – you know who I'm talkin' about, Miss Millicent. Keeps me on me Marylins, I can tell you.'

'Marylins?' asks Spencer.

Lottie taps the toe of the shoe. 'Marylin Monroes. Cockney rhymin' slang – means toes.'

'Sounds like Miss Lottie's from my neck of the woods,' says Mr Stubbs. 'Her Ladyship likes the box to be 'arder than some – layers and layers of 'essian and glue go into those.'

'You mean Perkins, don't you, Heart Maker? She's in the shop wiv Mrs Huntley-Palmer.'

Mr Stubbs taps his nose. 'Don't you say I said nothin' or I'll be in trouble with 'Er Upstairs.' The staircase groans. 'That'll be 'er, now. I should be gettin' on.'

'Heart Maker,' calls Mrs Huntley-Palmer. 'I'm ready for our clients now. Have you got Miss Perkins's shoes down there?'

'I'll take them up,' I say.

'Right you are. Good to see you again, miss.'

'You too, Mr Stubbs.'

'You take care now – it's a terrible pity what 'appened at the Scarlet Slippers, but accidents 'appen. Your mum was convinced you was goin' to bring back a trophy, she said as much that very mornin'.'

Under the stairs, Pip drops his hammer and nurses his thumb.

My heart hammers in my ears. 'You saw her, Mr Stubbs?'

'Came in to place an order, she did. She'd be pleased as punch to see you in a pair of *pointes* again. Don't you let nothin' or *no one* stop you from dancin'.'

8

Cinderella and Other Fairy Stories

By the time we get back to school, it's time for supper. We all spill out of Ms Celia's car and watch Willow weave across thc courtyard. 'Don't fink we'll be seein' her in the refectory tonight,' says Lottie. 'Fought we were going to hit that double-decker, miss. Never done a wheelie before!'

Ms Celia pats Winifred's bonnet. 'In thirty years of driving, the only thing I've hit is the brakes.'

'I take it all back,' says Spencer. 'Old Winnie's faster than my father's Ferrari. So when do we get to drive?'

'Year nine,' answers Ms Celia. 'However, there is an ocassional exception to the rule.'

Spencer pushes up his sunglasses. 'When do I start?'

The refectory isn't like the boring old canteen in St Tilda's. Sunbeams dapple the deep-blue walls and dance on the chandeliers. I can almost imagine how it feels to be a swan gliding across the lake.

Lottie sees my expression. 'It's the old ballroom, ain't it?'

'Home from home,' says Spencer, heading for the counter. 'I'm starved. What's the tuck like, Li? Our cook at home is a cordon bleu chef.'

Lottie thinks for a second. 'Mrs Toppin's more cordon blurghhh than cordon bleu.'

'Where do the teachers sit?' I ask.

'Don't see the teachers in here much. Cook's nosh is a bit *rich* for them.'

Spencer lifts the lid of a silver dome and stumbles back.

'What's the matter?'

'It's grey. I've never seen grey food before.'

Lottie moves along the counter. 'It's mashed potato but I'd stick to the noodles, if I was you. They ain't as good as my dad's but I ain't chucked up yet.'

'Did you say Mrs Topping? Is she related to Topsy?' I ask.

'Yeah, Cook's her mum.'

Spencer stares into a vat of bubbling grey worms. 'Explains everything.'

I pick up a bread roll and practise my new unreadable spy-face. 'Oh well, these look nice.'

'She's lyin',' says Lottie.

'You're right,' says Spencer. 'Looks like she needs all the practice she can get.'

We take our plates to a big round table with a stiff white cloth and proper napkins. Lottie tucks one under her chin and Spencer bangs down a bread roll. 'I could single-handedly take on Ivan Korolev with one of these,' he says. 'No offence,' he adds to the virtual Ivan, who's sitting next to him.

'None taken, Benedict.'

'So what have we got tomorrow?'

Ivan recites the timetable. 'Every morning your varm-up vill be followed by a two-hour rehearsal. After lunch, you vill study Spy Craft vith the Captain. There are more rehearsals in the evenings.'

'When's our free time?' I ask.

Ivan frowns. 'I'm sorry, I do not understand. Vhat is *free time*?'

Spencer blinks at his mentor. 'It's what you do when you're not working – you know, for fun?'

Ivan flickers. 'I'm sorry, I do not understand. Please repeat the qvestion.'

'Never mind that,' says Lottie. 'I'll tell you why he

was expelled if you turn him off. Don't feel right talkin' about him in front of his face.'

Ivan vanishes and Lottie wipes her chin. 'Poisoned the other finalists at the Scarlet Slippers. Then, *pwff*, disappeared. We was lucky Ms Celia's got antidotes for everyfink. When he showed up a few years ago, he'd started a ballet school like Swan House but for kids wiv form, if you know what I'm sayin'.'

'Form?' I ask.

'Crims, you know. *Criminals* – kids who've been in trouble – like him.'

'I don't get it,' says Spencer. 'What's the big deal if no one died? There's nothing wrong with being competitive.'

'*Competitive?* Is that what you call cheatin' in Chelsea? Korolev's the main reason Swan House ain't entered the Scarlet Slippers for so long.'

My Swanphone glows on my wrist. Spencer and Lottie check theirs too. 'They've posted our dorms,' says Spencer. 'I'm off to bags the best bed.'

'Who are you sharing with?' I ask.

'Mr Special and Danny Somebody. See you, Kydd.' Spencer flings his jacket over his shoulder. 'You too, Shorty.'

Lottie watches him jog across the refectory. 'Not if I see him first. If he was half as cool as he finks he is, he'd have a carrot for a nose. And if he calls me

Shorty one more time, I'll . . . Milly, what's wrong?'

I feel like I've got bubblegum stuck in my windpipe. The pictures on my Swanphone are of Willow Perkins and her friend, Bumble.

'Are you sure that's right?' I ask my Swanphone.

'Of course. I'm the smartest device on the planet.'

'Tell me you ain't got Perkins?' says Lottie.

'And Bumble. Is her real name Amy Bee?'

'Yeah. Look, Topsy's over there.' She points at the counter. 'Ask her if you can swap dorms. I'm wiv Dipti and Fleur. Fleur's friends wiv Perkins, she won't mind.' Lottie pushes back her chair. 'Sorry, Milly. Got to go. It's time for my tellin' off wiv Madame. She'll kill me if I'm late.'

I've been so busy thinking about my problems I'd forgotten about Madame. I wish Lottie luck and she shrugs it off. I have never met anyone like Lottie Li.

Topsy is hoovering up the leftovers. She looks up from a vat of custard and waves me over. 'Sho yummy. Wish I could cook like Mumsie, but I can't boil an *oeuf*.' She honks. 'Anyhooo – is everything all right, Milly?'

For one horrible moment I think I'm going to cry.

'Oh, Milly, what's the matter? You can tell me *anything*, you know – that's what Mummy Swans are for. Well, as long as it isn't classified. It isn't classified, is it?'

'I don't think so. Topsy, *please* could you put me in a different dorm?'

Topsy looks puzzled. 'But you're with Willow, aren't you? I thought you two were old besties?'

I bite my lip to stop it wobbling.

'I'm ever so sorry, Milly, I have to pass my probation before I'm allowed to organize the dorms. You need to speak to Madame – *eek*. Don't look so glum. Come on, I'll take you to her study.'

I plod across the refectory. After this morning, I can't see Madame doing me any favours.

Madame's room is opposite Dame Anna's statue. 'I'm sure Madame won't mind, but better touch her for luck,' says Topsy, nodding at the statue. 'Wait here and I'll go and explain.'

Lottie is leaving as Topsy lets herself in. Her cheeks dimple when she sees me. 'What are you doin' here?'

'I've got to ask Madame if I can swap dorms. Are you OK?'

'Yeah. She's in a good mood for once. Just got to watch my p's and q's for a bit. Fingers crossed, we'll be sharin' a dorm tomorrow.'

I stand outside Madame's room and catch the words *dorm*, and *Milly*, and *teary*.

Topsy gives me a double thumbs up on her way out.

When I go in, Madame is frowning at her Swanphone and doesn't look up. 'Zere is a late delivery I must attend to. Sit down and touch nothing.'

Apart from a grandfather clock and a lovely old cabinet in the corner, everything in Madame's room is white. I sit on a hard wooden chair and stand up again.

What am I going to do if Madame won't let me swap with Fleur?

I start pacing in front of the cabinet. How many more lies will Willow spread about me if we have to share a dorm?

A flash of scarlet and gold stops me in my tracks. Behind the glass of the cabinet is a red satin *pointe* shoe mounted on a shiny gold base. It's a Scarlet Slipper trophy just like Mum's. But where Mum's is engraved with *Eva Lilova*, this one says *Olga Popova*. I wonder if Olga Popova is Filipp's mum.

The trophy is surrounded by old ballet shoes, flowery tiaras and a big leather photograph album. Stuck on the front is a picture of the Popov dynasty. The family is posing on the lawn of a snooty sort of house with more windows than I can count. Pressed against an upstairs window are the blurry features of a little boy.

I touch the cabinet. It's Filipp Popov. All alone. My insides twang like a broken string.

Ms Celia pops her head around the door. 'Oh,

Milly, it's you. I was just looking for Madame.'

I drop my hand and my fingers leave smudgy prints on the glass. 'She had to do something. She told me to wait.'

Ms Celia joins me at the cabinet. 'Filipp Popov is your mentor, isn't he?'

'Yes, but I don't know why. He doesn't like me very much.'

'Filipp doesn't have feelings, Milly, he's just a hologram.'

'I wish someone would tell him that.'

'To be frank, Filipp was always a difficult boy. He found criticism rather hard to take. I'm afraid he didn't do terribly well.'

'Did the Popovs know he was a spy?'

'Heavens no. They thought he was simply training to be a dancer. Sadly, that didn't work out.'

'What happened to him?'

'I have no idea, Milly. Dame Anna and his mother, Olga, refuse to talk about him. I think he must have fallen out of love with ballet. I did wonder if that's why you were paired together.' I find out that when Ms Celia looks straight at you, it's impossible to look away.

'I could never fall out of love with ballet, Ms Celia. But sometimes I think ballet's fallen out of love with me.'

Ms Celia gives me her lightning smile. 'Even if that was the case, you're here now. You have an opportunity to start afresh.'

Isn't that what Bab said? 'I suppose so. Why are the Popovs' things here? If I won a Scarlet Slipper I wouldn't part with it for all the shoes in Meekes.'

'They have many more at home. Dame Anna donated the cabinet to the school as a thank you for giving Filipp a place. I believe some of the items are quite valuable – Madame's most treasured possessions, in fact. Why are you waiting for her? You're not in trouble, I hope?'

'Oh no. I just wanted to ask if I could swap dorms.'

'Honestly, Milly, I thought you'd have risen above that nonsense with Willow Perkins by now. You should be putting petty jealousies behind you. Remember, there are far more important things to worry about at Swan House.'

My head droops. That's easy for her to say, but she doesn't know Willow Perkins like I do.

Her voice softens. 'When you threw yourself in front of the Spencers' car this morning, you demonstrated many of the qualities you'll need to succeed at Swan House. If you work hard, you could do very well. Right, I must go. Tell Madame I called in, would you? I'll speak with her later.'

When Madame returns, she finds me with my nose pressed against the cabinet. Her fingernails tap the desk as I hurry back to the chair.

'Millicent –' *tap, tap, tap* – 'Miss Topping tells me zat you are unhappy with your dorm. Why is zat?'

'I'd like to share with Lottie, Madame. I could swap with Fleur Fontaine – Willow and Amy would rather share with her anyway.'

'*Au contraire*. Willow was most pleased with ze arrangement.'

'She was?'

'*Absolument*. She is such a forgiving child. Zere is much you could learn from her. In fact, think of zis as an opportunity to make up for ze way you have treated Willow in ze past.'

'But Madame—'

'Goodnight, Millicent, I have no more to say on ze matter.'

I close the door quietly and wander over to Dame Anna's statue. I brush her arm with my fingertips and wish for luck. I've never needed it more.

'Cooo-ee! Milly . . .' Topsy galumphs alongside me. 'What did Madame say?'

'I have to stay where I am.'

Topsy puffs her hair out of her eyes. 'Oh well, I'm sure Madame knows best. We should be tucked up in Bedfordshire by now. I'll show you to your dorm.'

Outside, a row of carriage lights twinkles in the darkness. I follow Topsy along a covered walkway that leads to the coach house. The wisteria glows in the moonlight. Through the archway there's a horseshoe of brick outbuildings. I can't see the trees beyond, but I can hear them whisper in the breeze.

'Here we are, the old stable block. Girls on this side. Boys on the other.'

An owl hoots in the distance and Topsy shudders. 'Spooky, isn't it? You never know who's going to creep out of the woods or crawl out of the lake. That's why Ms Celia takes security sooo seriously. Look, she gave me *this*.'

I back away as Topsy pulls something shiny from her pocket. The metal glints in her hand. 'It's OK, I've had special training.' She tugs a referee's whistle over her hair. 'The doors are all alarmed so the only people who can enter are you and your roomies.'

'But I haven't got a key.'

'You don't need one. As long as you're wearing your Swanphone and Ms Celia's given you clearance, you can come and go as you please. If you need me, I'm in the dorm in the middle.' She points along the line of stable doors. 'Anyhooo, don't have too much fun, will you? I was always getting into scrapes when I was little.'

'You studied here?'

Topsy snorts. 'No, *obvs* – Mummy's been the cook since Daddy died. So O let me live here too.'

'Who's O?'

'He's Ms Celia's boss, but no one ever sees him. *Eek,* is that the time? Nightie night, Milly, mind the bugs don't bite.' She snorts again. 'Just my little spy joke. *Bugs*. Bugs? No?' Gripping her whistle, Topsy hurries to her room.

I press my ear against the door and hear muffled voices inside. Why would Willow tell Madame she was happy for me to share her dorm? I listen carefully.

'Look at this . . .' Willow's saying.

'What?'

'THIS. The *lump* on my elbow. It's from the Scarlet Slippers when Milly Kydd pushed me over.'

'She's so vile.'

'I know. And *this* is worse.'

'The mark on your knee?'

'The *scar* on my knee. Milly did it when we were in Ballet Tots. She was jealous because I was Cinderella and she was just a pumpkin. Even when we were little, everyone knew *I* was the gifted one. Her mum said I had the potential to be the next Anna Popova.'

My throat aches. The first bit's a lie, but everything else is true. Willow was better than me and Mum knew it.

I try to squash the memory down, but it's no good. When I close my eyes, there I am onstage. A small girl in a puffed-up pumpkin tutu, wearing a garland of floppy leaves in my hair and a scowl that stretches from one green ear to the other.

Just below the stage, Mr Lamont plays the piano and I begin my pumpkin dance.

Behind the set, where only I can see, a smaller girl in Cinders' rags copies my every move. I twirl like a pumpkin, she twirls like a princess. I jump like a pumpkin, she jumps like a princess. I land like a pumpkin – *she trips over the set*.

Mr Lamont plays her cue.

'Hurry up, Willow,' I whisper. The hand I reach for is hot and trembly. I spin us around. 'Faster, Willow, do it like we practised.' But Willow's feet are stuck.

'I can't,' she says. 'My leg is hurting.'

'You'll spoil *everything*!' I scold. 'Come on, you have to change into your party dress behind the screen.' I start to skip, dragging her behind me.

When we emerge, Willow's not in her party dress; she's in tears. I am one extremely cross pumpkin. As she collapses, I fold my arms. I even do a little stomp.

All the parents watching begin to mutter. Chairs shuffle. Mum is the first to reach us.

'What's the matter, Willow? Are you hurt?'

'It's my leg,' moans Willow.

Mum lifts Willow's Cinder skirt. Her tights are pink with blood.

'Goodness, that looks painful,' says Mum. 'What happened?'

'It was Milly,' says Willow.

I open my mouth. '*What?*'

Willow sucks her thumb. 'Milly did it when we were behind the screen.'

Mum's face turns ever so pale. 'Someone had better call a doctor. Where's your mummy, Willow?'

'I haven't got a mummy.'

'Your daddy?'

'He doesn't like dancy things.'

'You poor little mite. Come on, sweetheart. Let's make you better . . .'

I thought that would be it. The End. But it wasn't. I never knew who Mum really believed that day, but Willow carried on lying and Mum carried on making her better. Right up until the day she disappeared.

I press my ear back against the door. Behind the door, Willow prattles on. 'After that, Eva gave me extra lessons. Then when she disappeared, Madame spotted my talent too. She even let me start the term early so Daddy could get back to work.'

I can't believe it. Now that Willow's got Madame wrapped around her little finger, she doesn't need

Mum any more. My Swanphone glows red. 'Alert. The increase in your heart rate and decrease in your cortisol levels indicate that you're about to do, or say, something you'll regret. Your anger is most likely a symptom of fatigue. It is now twenty-two hundred hours. Your first ballet class is at zero nine hundred hours and the *minimum* amount of sleep required for optimum performance is—'

I slip it off my wrist and put it in my pocket. I don't need a Swanphone to tell me when I'm angry.

There's a SHHHH as I enter the dorm.

Willow and Bumble are sitting on their beds. 'Did you have a nice little talk with Madame?' says Willow.

'How did you know about that?'

'She messaged me to say you didn't want to share with us. That's not very nice, is it, Bumble?'

'We were quite hurt,' says Bumble. 'Especially as we'd unpacked for you and everything.'

Willow smiles sweetly. 'I wanted to make up for that silly prank earlier so I made up your bed too.' I look at the suitcases piled high on the third bed. 'Not that one, silly, it's through there.'

My anger fizzles out. This is the first nice thing she's ever done for me. Maybe she is a little bit sorry?

There's a door leading to an adjoining room. I trip over my slippers. My trunk lies on its side. Everything else I own is in the bath. The shower head is still dripping.

Bumble giggles. 'Some of it was a bit smelly so we gave it a wash.'

A furry ginger tail hangs out of the loo. I cry out, 'Boris!' I rescue my hot-water bottle Boris and slam the door.

Sorry? Willow Perkins doesn't know the meaning of the word.

9

The Shoe Keeper

I wake up with a damp, furry hot-water bottle on my cheek.

Where am I? The pale-blue ceiling is painted with fluffy, white clouds. Light leaks through the shutters. Across the room, two bodies are snuggled under their quilts.

My heart sinks into the mattress.

Today I have my first ballet class. Two hours of Willow being Cinderella. Two hours of me being a pumpkin.

I pull on some leggings and a T-shirt and tiptoe outside. In the morning light, the courtyard doesn't look spooky at all. Shutters cover the windows. Hanging baskets brim with pansies. Sunlight winks through the trees behind the stables. There's a rustle behind me, but it's only a blackbird in the treetops.

Waiting on the reception desk is a delivery from

Meekes. I unstack the shoeboxes and find mine on the bottom. Stamped on the soles of my *pointe* shoes are my initials and little black hearts. I press the satin against my cheek.

Perfect.

When I get back to the dorm, Willow and Bumble have gone for breakfast, so I sit on my bed and prepare my *pointe* shoes just like Mum used to. I sew on the ribbons and elastic. Slice and bend the soles. Then bash each box until it's just right. Happy with my work, I leave them at the end of my bed and go to find Lottie.

I spot her jogging across the courtyard, already dressed in her practice clothes. 'I was just comin' to get you. What happened last night?'

Over breakfast, I tell her about my meeting with Madame, but I don't mention what happened with Willow and my things. Lottie will get mad and the last thing I want to do is get her into more trouble.

She throws down her spoon. 'Why won't Madame let you swap dorms? It's no skin off her nose.'

'I don't know. I'll just have to avoid Willow somehow.'

Lottie nods at the door. 'Look, she's headin' for class. You're safe to get changed now.'

Back in the dorm, I wriggle into my new tights and leotard, roll on my stripy leg warmers, and scrunch my hair into a pea-sized bun. I fug the room with hairspray, then grope the floor for my shoes.

I peep under my bed. Look in my trunk. Glance at my wrist.

'Eight forty-eight,' says my Swanphone. 'Twelve minutes until your class with Madame.'

Willow and Bumble must have hidden my shoes. I look under their beds. Nothing.

I start rifling through Willow's clothes. No shoes in her cupboard. Blimey, how many leg warmers does a two-legged girl need?

Rifle, rifle – drat.

I run back to reception, but all the boxes have gone and there's no one to ask.

Five minutes until class.

I sprint back to the dorm.

'Your class with Madame will begin in three minutes,' says my Swanphone. 'I suggest you leave now.'

What should I do? Lottie said Madame hates people to be late, but I can't go to class without shoes. Then I remember my mentor.

Filipp Popov leaps onto my trunk. I suppose it's easier to look down his see-through mousey nose at me from up there. 'What do you want?' he snaps.

'I've got a class with Madame, but I've lost my new shoes.'

Filipp taps his sticky-out teeth with his finger. 'Let me think.'

'Please can you think a bit faster?'

'Sorry, I am unable to process your request . . . would you like me to reboot?'

'NO! I mean, no thank you – just tell me what I should do.'

'Have you been to the Shoe Keeper?'

'The Shoe Keeper – who's that?'

'You haven't met Madge Little?' Filipp jumps off the trunk and stumbles to the door. 'I'll take you to her cupboard.'

Her *cupboard*?

I watch my mentor *jeté* clumsily across the courtyard. At this rate, I'll never get to Madame's class.

'Please just tell me where this Madge person is, and I'll find her myself.'

'Suit yourself. She's on the first floor. Go right at the top of the stairs.'

I take the stairs two at a time. The door isn't locked, so I push straight in.

The Shoe Keeper's room is musty and lined with cubby holes. Every inch is crammed with shoeboxes. Propped against the back wall is a little ladder. At the top, a pair of flowery curtains is drawn across a human-size cubby hole. The curtains flutter – someone is snoring inside.

'Hello? Miss Little, are you there?'

There's a *hrmph*.

'Miss Little?' No answer. '*Madge?*'

A face peeps between the curtains. Madge Little has a snubbed pink nose and the worried expression of a guinea pig.

'What time is it? Who are you? Do you have an appointment?'

'It's five past nine and I'm Milly Kydd and no I don't, but it's an emergency.'

'Emergency? What are you here for? Shoes or –' Madge Little lowers her voice – '*doobries*?'

'Uhh . . . shoes? Definitely shoes.'

'Sorry, I'm busy.' The curtains snap closed.

'Miss Little, please – I've lost my new shoes and I've got a class right now this very minute.'

'Who with?' she asks from behind the curtain.

'Madame.'

'What did you say your name was?'

'Milly. Milly Kydd.'

There's a scrabbling noise, then Madge scoots down the ladder. Her streaky grey hair sticks up on one side and her winceyette nightie's inside out.

'Madame won't like you being late. Not one little bit. What did you need?' She scurries along the row of boxes.

'A pair of size fours,' I say. 'As quickly as possible,

please.'

'Size fours, did you say? Oh dear. Oh no. Got me out of bed at six o'clock, she did, and took every pair of size fours I had. And did she say thank you, Miss Little, sorry to disturb you, Miss Little? No, she did not.'

'Who? Who took all the shoes?'

'Miss Perkins. Do you know her? You could ask her to lend you a pair.'

Willow. I can't let her get away with it this time. 'I'll take a pair of size fives, please.'

'You are eight minutes late for class,' says my Swanphone.

'Oh dear. The fives are all out.' Madge Little reaches for one of the cubby holes. 'I've got a pair of three and a halfs, but they won't do your feet any good.'

'I suppose they'll have to do – but please can you hurry!'

By the time I skid into Madame's studio, I'm not late. I'm history.

Twenty pairs of eyes look up from the barre. Sunlight streams through the windows and bounces off a wall of mirrors. Willow Perkins smirks at my reflection. My hair's escaped. My face is pink and worried. I could be Madge Little's guinea-pig daughter.

Madame doesn't bat a pearly eyelid in my direction. 'Charlotte, zis is ze ballet not ze boxing. Now ze other side. Same arm as your working leg.'

A lady in a cardigan and thick, brown tights thumps at the piano. Madame holds up her hand and the music stops. She turns to me. 'You are late.'

'Sorry, Madame, I lost my sh—'

Madame waves her hand impatiently. 'If I want an excuse, I will ask for an excuse. We follow one simple rule in my class, and it is zis: if *one* person is late, *everyone* is punished. *Comprenez-vous?*' Twenty pairs of eyes roll in my direction. 'I said, do you understand?'

'Yes, Madame.'

'Class, as Millicent missed ze warming-up, you will *all* start from ze beginning. So, attention –' she demonstrates a combination of steps – 'Begin with *battement tendu devant*. Zen *de côté*. Zen *derrière*. Close to first and repeat *de côté*. Finish in first with your arms in *bras bas* and repeat on the other side.'

My head is spinning and I haven't even started yet.

She waves at the piano. '*Music*, Mademoiselle Batty.'

It's been eight months since I've been to a ballet class. By the time I'm *tenduing devant* everyone else is *tenduing derrière*. I wipe the sweat from my eyes.

Willow isn't even glowing.

'Keep up, Millicent!' snaps Madame. 'Ze other leg! Now balance . . . hold . . . hold . . . and *finis*!'

The balls of my feet are great balls of fire.

'G-golly,' says Miss Batty. 'It's a qu-quarter past ten, Madame.'

'I am aware of ze hour, mademoiselle.'

'But isn't it t-time for our little b-break?'

'*Break*, mademoiselle? Do you forget why zese children are here? Will zey have a *little break* when zey are under ze cover? Will zey have a *little break* when zey are interrogated and tortured? Pah! Go for a cup of your precious English tea. Everyone else will stay until *she* –' she points at me – 'is perfect!'

Even Lottie groans. Miss Batty gathers her music in her arms. Sheets fly as she scurries across the studio.

Madame claps her hands. 'Girls, change into your *pointe* shoes. *Vite!*'

I grit my teeth as I change from my teeny-tiny flats into my teeny-tiny *pointe* shoes.

Madame hovers over me. 'What is taking you so long, Millicent? I do not comprehend. Why are you wearing shoes zat are too small? You are like one of Cinderella's ugly sisters, *non*?'

Everyone laughs.

'I lost my shoes, Madame. These were the only size the Shoe Keeper had.' I spot Willow's face in the mirror. All violet eyes and innocence.

'I do not tolerate excuses in my class.'

I bite my lip. 'Sorry, Madame. I'm ready now.'

'Zen to ze centre, if you please. Your mother made her name in *Swan Lake*, did she not?'

Twenty pairs of eyes watch me hobble to the centre. 'Yes, Madame.'

'People say she made thirty-two *fouetté* turns look – how do you say – *easy-peasy*.'

'Yes, Madame. She was amazing.'

'You are lucky to have a mother who could teach you so much. I suppose she taught you to perform ze perfect *fouetté*?'

A voice whispers in my head. A velvety voice that conjures up tutus and tiaras.

Clever girl, Milly, that was so, so close. Just try one more time . . .

'Yes, Madame.'

'Excellent. Now you will show us all what you have learnt.'

I glance down. My toes are sticky with blood.

Mum whispers through the pain.

You can do it, sweetheart. Start in fourth.

I stand in fourth position.

It's all about your supporting leg, remember? Now lift your chest and passé.

I lift my chest and *passé*.

Find your spot and spin. Move your arm and leg like they're on a string.

I find my spot and spin, but my toes are on fire. On my second *fouetté*, I teeter. On the third, I totter. On the fourth, my toes fold and I tumble to the floor.

'A pity,' says Madame. 'But it is only to be expected.'

Willow Perkins shoots up her hand. 'Madame, Eva Kydd taught me too. *I* can show you her method.'

'Thank you, Willow, please do.'

With every perfect *fouetté*, I hear Mum's voice. *Beautiful, Willow. Did you see, Milly, how well Willow is doing . . .*

Mum taught her brilliantly.

Madame applauds. '*Bien*. If only Ms Celia had chosen *you* to dance in the ze Scarlet Slippers, Willow.'

A mumble travels along the barre.

'What do you mean, Madame?' says Willow.

'As you know, each of ze schools must perform three times. Zis year, ze dances are taken from variations from *Ze Sleeping Beauty, Romeo and Juliet* and *Swan Lake*. Ms Celia has decided zat just one person will lead for Swan House in all three dances . . .'

The mumble turns to a rumble. Madame circles the room.

'Who's that?' says Willow.

Madame stops next to the piano and carefully closes the lid. 'Class, please join me in congratulating our new principal dancer . . . *Millicent Kydd*.'

10

The Dance of Death

At lunchtime, I try to concentrate on my food but it's not easy with everyone staring and Spencer groaning, 'I can't believe the mission hangs on *Kydd*,' between every mouthful.

'Shut up, Spence,' says Lottie.

'It's all right, Lottie,' I say. 'I honestly don't know what Ms Celia was thinking. I thought she wanted us to do well?'

'Exactly. *Or lives will be lost* and all that.' Spencer jabs his fork into the slice of rubber on his plate. 'Thought this was supposed to be beef Wellington.'

'More like wellington boot,' says Lottie.

I push away my plate. 'I really, really need to see Ms Celia right now, this very minute.'

Spencer puts down his fork. 'She's gone out. Saw her take off in Winifred like she was off to save the world.'

'Then what am I going to do? You saw me in class.

I can't even do a *fouetté*!'

'It ain't your fault you fell over, Milly,' says Lottie. 'Blame Perkins. Your shoes was too small.'

I groan. 'And what's Madge going to say? There's blood all over her three and a halfs.'

'That's nuffink,' says Lottie. 'Last term I mistimed a karate chop and broke the Captain's nose. Should have seen him wiv a pink beard. He looked like a giant My Little Pony.'

Spencer grins. 'Cheer up, we've got Spy Craft next. That's going to be so cool.'

We give up on our wellington boots and head upstairs to the gym. At the top of the staircase, I glimpse Ms Celia's Hall of Fame. Didn't Topsy say there were lasers up here? I stay as close as possible to Lottie.

The gym has rows of leather punch bags and targets on the walls. Waiting next to a dummy hanging from the ceiling is the Captain. He's swapped his suit and tie for a karate suit and a bag full of headguards and boxing gloves.

The double doors swing open and in walks Merv. I don't think he's going to need his satchel.

'Listen up, you lot,' says the Captain. 'It's just twelve weeks until Korolev shows up, so here's the deal . . .' He rubs his beardy jaw. 'No crying – I can't be doing with tears. No backchat – you'll do what you're told, no questions asked. And no whinging – I especially can't be doing with whinging.'

'Why's he looking at me?' says Merv.

'As a few of you are new, we'll start with a basic warm-up. Everyone grab a mat.'

Turns out the Captain's warm-ups are worse than Madame's. The next hour consists of an unnecessary amount of shouting (the Captain) and an unnatural amount of puffing (me). I finish my bottle of water in the first five minutes and survive the rest of the class by licking the sweat off my top lip.

When the torture stops, I collapse on the mat. Only one person looks worse than me. In fact, it is entirely possible that Merv is dead. The Captain checks his pulse before prodding him in the back with a big hairy foot.

'Get up, son. We've only just begun.'

Merv moans and rolls over. 'When am I ever going to have to deliver a killer blow to the solar plexus? Martial arts are a waste of time if you're never going to work in the field, and believe me, I am *never* going to work in the field. I'm genetically unsuited to physical combat. My skills are cerebral.'

The Captain pulls Merv to his feet. 'Pass the practical part of this course or you'll be out on your *cerebrum*. Don't laugh, Spencer, Merv's not the only one who'd better watch out. In the run up to the Scarlet Slippers, you will all be monitored continually. Right, before we move on, are there any questions?'

I wonder what 'monitored continually' means. Does it mean someone watches us *all the time*? Like, even when we're *on the loo*?

I put my hand up and ask.

The Captain rumbles, 'Anyone got any *sensible* questions?'

I put my hand up again. 'I have, but it's not sensible at all. Actually, it's the maddest thing I ever heard. Miss Topping said there were lasers in the school. She said they'd cut you in half if you didn't have clearance.' I laugh. *Ha-ha-ha.* 'There aren't really, are there? Lasers? That cut people in half?'

The Captain looks at me like I'm the mad one for asking.

Lottie whispers in my ear, 'They say there was this double agent once. Disguised herself as Ms Celia. Paisley scarf. Oxford bags. Engine grease under her nails. Dead ringer, she was, even the eyes. They say the lasers went clean fru' her. Had to bring in the specialists to clean her up.'

'Anyone else got any questions?' says the Captain. 'What now, Kydd?'

'Uhh, just one more.' I think it might be important. 'What's *clearance*?'

It's raining when the Captain gathers us in the courtyard. A group of bedraggled sixth years carries a stretcher away from the assault course. I overhear one boy say, 'It's not called the Dance of Death for nothing.'

Willow's chatting with a small boy who must think I'm a mentor, because he keeps trying to walk through me.

The Captain's beard drips onto his Viking chest. 'In case you haven't noticed, it's chucking it down, Spencer. You can lose the shades.' Spencer shrugs and puts his sunglasses in his pocket. 'Right, listen up, everyone – today we're going to kick off with evasion and tracking. Skills we may need to use when Korolev's school arrives.'

'Sounds easy enough to me,' says Spencer.

The Captain waggles a gnarled finger in his direction. 'Think you know it all already, son? In that case, you can be one of our marks. You too, Merv.'

'*Me?*' Merv's monobrow leaps so high it could win a Scarlet Slipper.

Lottie's eyes flick at Willow. 'Better stick wiv me, Milly . . .' Her Swanphone hums. 'Hang on, I've got a message.'

'What is it, Li?' asks the Captain.

Lottie chews her lip. 'I need to be excused. Got an OFA.'

'An OFA?' I ask.

'*Order From Above.*' She squeezes my arm. 'Don't like the way Willow and her gang are lookin' at you. Keep well out their way, all right?'

I nod but all my courage seems to pad away with Lottie's footsteps.

'Kydd, are you listening?' says the Captain.

'Uh?'

'Thought not. There's only one place daydreaming will get you in this line of work.' He points at the clouds. 'Switch off like that and you're dead. Garrick, tell Kydd what I just said, would you?'

The boy next to Willow says, 'You were asking for a third volunteer, Captain.'

The Captain grins. 'Well, done, Kydd – you just got yourself the job. The rest of you get into pairs. Your goal is to to track our three marks. Remember, this isn't hide and seek. Keep quiet. Keep out of sight. Marks – use your initiative. Trackers – keep your eyes open for evidence. Spencer, Merv, Kydd you've got a three minute head start. I want you *all* back here in one hour. Anyone who shows up late will find themselves on the Dance of Death.'

Willow's friend, Garrick, lasers me in half with his eyeballs.

'Three, two, one . . . *go*!'

'Split!' shouts Spencer, making for the school. Merv disappears through the archway. Garghhh. I panic and shoot off in the opposite direction.

Big mistake. Before I know it, I'm in the woods, stamping down brambles and pushing back branches. Dollops of rain plop through the leaves and drip off my nose. The air smells of wet cat.

There's a shout behind me. 'She went that way!' Footsteps stomp over the cobbles, then thump across the damp earth. So much for keeping quiet and out of sight.

I crash through the undergrowth, swiping at twigs and leaves.

Footsteps pound after me.

The path forks three ways. Which way do I go now? There's a whizz over my head. A branch above me crackles. A muffled laugh follows. Willow shouts out, 'Don't be stupid, Garrick. If the Captain catches you using the Zipper, he'll make us all do the Dance of Death!'

The Zipper? My heart *jetés*. I pull off my hoody. Hurl it down one track then follow another. The branches knit closer together. The path narrows until there is no path. I clamber over a fallen tree. Slide across the mossy bark. Hit the ground and choke back a cry. Not because of my burning toes, but because, right in front of me, is the lake.

A cold, grey, watery full stop.

Shivering, I wait for the footsteps. The catcalls. The Zipper. But the only sound is my raggedy breath and the pittery-pat of rain on the lake. No footsteps. No voices. No Willow.

I slide through the mud. Drawn up on the bank is a small, blue boat. Nestled under the trees behind it is a little hut. Somewhere to hide until the hour is up.

The door is stuck. I push as hard as I can and collapse inside.

But someone has beaten me to it.

11

The Secrets of Swan House

Instinctively I duck as a foot whizzes past my ear.

I scramble to my feet. 'Spencer! Stop!'

'Kydd?' Spencer drops his fists then holds his finger to his lips. 'Keep it down. Perkins and her gang are out there somewhere.'

'I know. Garrick just tried to Zip me. Is that bad?'

Spencer whistles. 'You remember the Captain said our Swanphones had inbuilt weapons systems? The Zipper's like a stun gun, only worse. You were lucky.'

Blimey.

I tug a twig out of my hair. 'How did you get here without being seen?'

'Same as you.'

'No, you didn't. That door hasn't been opened for ages.'

Spencer folds his arms. 'How do you think I got here?'

I turn around slowly. The window's too small to climb through and there aren't any holes in the roof. I stamp the boarded floor. Next to Spencer's foot is an old rug. I kick it back.

'No way. Is that a trap door?'

'Yes. This place is so cool. You'll never guess where it goes.'

My eyes run over Spencer's spotless trainers. His clean blue joggers. The bottoms of mine are a sludgy brown.

'The school! It goes to the school. You haven't even been in the woods, have you?'

'Well done, Bond. The door leads to a tunnel. Lots of them, in fact. Lord Whatshisname dug them when he built the house. Look.'

Spencer tugs on a rusty handle set into the floor and we both peer into the darkness. He shines his Swanphone down a winding stone staircase.

'How did you find out about this?' My voice is all echoey.

'Ivan. He found the tunnels when he was a student.'

'I'm surprised he's allowed to show you. Every time I ask Filipp a question, he tells me the answer's classified.'

'I asked Ivan about that. Apparently, he helped design the first ever MNTR program when he was at school and made some 'adjustments'. Don't tell Mr Special, will you? He'll spoil all my fun. So far, I've taken one tunnel that comes out in Madame's study and another that goes down to the lab where Madge Little develops her doobries.'

'Doobries? Are they something to do with shoes?'

Spencer grins. 'Madge's real job is making spy gadgets. You know, poisonous plasters and flying tutus.'

'Flying tutus? Don't be silly, Spencer. Anyway, how come you're allowed to go wandering around down there?'

'I'm not. That's why it's cool.'

'So why haven't you been caught?'

Spencer shrugs. 'I think the tunnels must be so secret there aren't any security cameras. Anyway, if you don't fancy facing the Dance of Death tonight, we'd better get back.' He lifts the trap door. 'You coming or taking the scenic route? Apart from Ivan, I've only seen one rat so far.'

'No thanks. Willow should have gone by now. I've got to find my hoody.'

I help Spencer slide the hatch over his blond head, then jog back to the fork in the path. I scour the forest floor, but my hoody's gone. A trail of footprints leads down a muddy track winding away from the lake.

There's a grunt behind me.

I spin around. A startled eyebrow jiggles in the shadows. 'Merv! You scared me. What are doing out here? I thought you went to the dorms.'

Merv looks like he's been crying. 'I panicked. Then I got lost and my Swanphone refused to help. Kydd, you've got to get me back in time. There's no way I'd survive the Dance of Death.'

I spot a patch of pale blue behind a tree. 'OK, I'll just grab my hoody.'

But as I get closer, my hoody twitches. A twig snaps under my foot.

'Who is it?' croaks a voice from behind the trunk.

I round the tree and see Garrick slumped under it. His face is green and pasty but he still manages to blush when he sees me. 'Oh. It's you.'

I hang back. 'Are you OK?'

'Went over on my ankle when we were running back, but the others just left me.' He grimaces. 'I think it's broken.'

'Someone else'll help him,' says Merv. 'Come on, Kydd. WE'RE TALKING ABOUT THE DANCE OF DEATH!'

Garrick clutches his ankle. 'Your mate's right. The Dance is no fun, believe me.' Thunder rumbles over the lake and he shivers.

Merv waves his wrist under my nose. 'The time,

Kydd. LOOK AT THE TIME!'

I turn to leave but Willow's voice whispers in my ear. *My leg is hurting*, it says. I ignored Willow back then and look where it got me.

'Sorry, Merv. We've got to help. I mean, the Dance of Death – how hard can it be?' I crouch down next to Garrick. 'Let's get you to the infirmary.'

By the time we've dropped Garrick at the infirmary, we're really, really late. The Captain frowns when he spots us tramping towards him. His Thor-sized shadow looms across the cobbles. 'Follow me.'

He takes me and a whimpering Merv past the obstacle course and keeps on walking. We slog away from the lake until he stops at a tall wooden fence post. 'The Dance of Death,' he says.

I gaze up. The fence stretches into the woods. Between the posts, barbed wire glints blood-red against the rust-coloured sky. 'I-I don't understand.'

'Don't you see, Kydd?' groans Merv. 'It's a test. We have to circumnavigate the school grounds.'

That doesn't sound so bad. It might take all night but it's not going to kill us.

'It's a test all right,' says the Captain. 'Of strength, endurance, balance and coordination. What Merv didn't mention is that the cirumnavigation takes place up there.'

'*What?*'

'You must dance from post to post. I don't need to tell you what'll happen if you make a mistake.'

The posts are a *jeté* apart. I won't last five minutes. Merv won't last one.

'I don't want to die,' says Merv.

The Captain's beard twitches. 'Then it's lucky you're both off the hook. Nurse told us you'd helped Garrick. But let this be a warning to you; we can't tolerate failure at Swan House – the stakes are too high.'

I take one last look at the top of the post. He can say that again.

It's really, really, *really* late when Merv and I limp into the refectory. Spencer's the only person in there. He waves us over to his table.

'Water, I need water,' says Merv.

'What's the matter with him?' says Spencer.

'I can't feel my face,' says Merv.

'Don't tell me you've done the Dance of Death?'

I explain about Garrick. 'We were lucky. The Captain let us off.'

Spencer digs in his bag. 'I don't understand why you helped Garrick. He tried to Zip you.'

'You'd have done the same thing, Spencer,' I say.

'No, he wouldn't,' says Merv.

'No, I wouldn't,' says Spencer. He hands me a sandwich. 'At least you missed supper. I think Cook mixed up her kippers with her slippers.'

I hand it back. 'Thanks, but I'm too tired to eat.'

'Thank Shorty – it was her idea. She'd have given it to you herself if she wasn't translating something.' Spencer tucks into the sandwich and picks something out of his teeth. He holds up a piece of orange string. 'String sandwich. Unusual, but strangely tasty.'

'What about me?' says Merv.

Spencer shrugs. 'What about you?'

'My blood sugars are dangerously low.'

'So you do eat!' says Spencer. 'I thought you were from that planet where aliens have no emotion and live purely on logic, like the guy with the pointy ears from *Star Trek*.'

Merv's tummy rumbles loud enough to prove that he is human, and probably from Devon, after all.

'You're in luck,' says Spencer. 'I've got some Fortnum's shortbread in my pocket. I've been keeping it for emergencies, but you can have it.'

'Is it vacuum packed?' says Merv.

Spencer pulls out a biscuit and picks off the fluff.

'Not exactly.'

Merv groans. 'Don't you think I've been through enough?'

I creep into my dorm expecting the worst. But my clothes are where I left them. My hot-water bottle Boris is still on my pillow. Willow and Bumble are pretending to be asleep.

Bumble opens one eye and snaps it shut again. Once I'm in bed, I'm too tired to think about Garrick or Zippers or what Willow might do next. I snuggle up to my hot-water bottle, say goodnight to Mum and Bab and the real Boris, wherever they are, and seconds later, I'm dreaming about boats and lakes and dances of death.

12

The Fall of the White Swan

The next morning at breakfast, Willow is looking even more pleased with herself that usual. Probably because we've got Madame and we both know how that's going to go. Why oh why did Ms Celia decide it would be a good idea to give me all the lead roles?

'Don't worry about Perkins,' says Lottie. 'Now the Captain's said we're being monitored continually, she wouldn't dare try nuffink dodgy.'

'I hope you're right,' I say. 'I wonder if anyone saw her stealing my ballet shoes?' My Swanphone glows. 'Ooo, speaking of shoes, my new ones have arrived from Meekes.'

'That was quick,' says Spencer.

'Topsy ordered them yesterday. I've got a blood blister where my little toe used to be.'

'Do you mind, Kydd?' Spencer prods his egg. 'I'm

trying to eat my scrambled brains.'

'Sorry, Spencer.' I pick up my bag. 'See you both in class.'

I spot Heart Maker's apprentice before he spots me. He's ogling Dame Anna's statue and smiles when he sees me. 'Hello, miss. I need someone to sign for these boxes, if you don't mind?' The pad in his hand is shaking.

'Are you all right? I ask.

Pip laughs. 'I'm fine, just a bit shaken, that's all. Had a tumble on the stairs at Meekes this morning. It's been a bit of a week, what with Star Maker standing on a craft-knife, then Heart Maker almost electrocuting himself.'

'*Mr Stubbs?* What happened?'

'The kettle blew up. Don't worry, miss, he had a narrow escape.'

Thank goodness. Now Bab's gone, Mr Stubbs is my only link with Mum. I couldn't bear it if something happened to him.

'Hellooo!' I jump as Topsy taps my shoulder. 'Sorry about that. Been with the yoga teacher. Poor thing pulled her gluteous minimus doing the one-legged pigeon.' She counts the boxes. ' . . . eleven, twelve, thirteen – *eek* – unlucky for some. What's the matter, Pip? You're not coming down with something, are you?'

'Pip fell down the stairs at work,' I say.

'Oh, Pip. You poor thing,' says Topsy. 'Come on, let's get you a cup of cocoa. Off you go to class now, Milly. I'll take care of him.'

Her '*there-there*'s follow me all the way to Madame's studio.

When I arrive at the studio door, everyone is following Ms Celia into the corridor. Lottie calls me over. 'Sorry, Milly, Ms Celia's teachin' the *corps de ballet* while you're wiv Madame.'

'Hurry now, Milly, Madame does not like to be kept waiting,' says Ms Celia.

I hold the studio door open for Miss Batty. 'Thank you, M-Milly. T-time to face the m-music . . .'

Danny Debello, Willow and an older boy are already stretching at the barre. Willow raises her leg and touches her knee with her nose. I wish I was still that bendy.

Madame claps her hands. 'So good of you to join us, Millicent. Today we will be rehearsing a *pas de deux* for ze Scarlet Slippers. Daniel has bravely agreed to partner you. As you can see, we have been joined by Willow and Dafydd also. In ze event zat one of you should get injured, zey will take your place.'

I feel my face redden. Willow's dance partner is only Dafydd Wynn-Jones. Head boy and all-round superstar.

Madame smiles at everyone except me. 'Now, who can tell me what makes ze perfect dance partnership?'

'Height?' says Willow.

'*Oui*. Height is important.'

'Respect,' says Dafydd Wynn-Jones.

'Absolutely,' I say, a little too loudly. Willow rolls her eyeballs.

'And ze most important thing of all?' asks Madame.

'Trust, Madame,' says Danny.

'Well done, Daniel. Did you hear zat, Millicent? *Trust*. So, to begin, we will build trust between you and Daniel in a series of exercises. First, you will stand in fifth *en face* and allow Daniel to take your weight.'

My heart hiccups. Danny was one of the boys chasing me in the woods. It's going to take more than an exercise to make me trust him.

'Millicent, what are you waiting for?'

I take a breath as Danny holds me at the waist. Following Madame's instructions, he tilts me forward, back and side-to-side.

After three more exercises, I begin to relax.

'*Bien*, Daniel,' says Madame. 'Ze judges like to see lifts, so we shall give zem lifts. Zere are four in ze piece from *Swan Lake* I have chosen for you. However, we shall begin with something simple. A fish dive, perhaps?'

Lifts? I wipe my palms on my tights.

'What parts are we playing?' asks Danny.

'Your role is Von Rothbart, ze evil sorcerer, and Millicent will play Odette, ze tragic white swan. You are ready, Daniel?'

'Yes, Madame.'

'Millicent, do not look so scared. You are in good hands. Begin in *arabesque en pointe*.'

Danny wraps one arm around my waist and the other around my leg. He begins to tilt me downwards.

'Now bend your standing leg into a *passé*,' says Madame. 'Use your core to pull yourself into a line so your chin tilts towards ze floor.'

I tighten my stomach, but Danny's grip loosens. I tense my back, but he lets me slide. I yelp as my chin thumps the floor.

For a moment, I can't breathe. I taste blood on my tongue.

'*Non, non, non!*' shouts Madame. 'If your core is weak, how can Daniel be expected to hold you?'

'Sorry, Milly. Are you hurt?' Danny holds out his hand to help me up, but his eyes aren't sorry. His lips aren't sorry.

'Pah!' says Madame. 'Zere is nothing wrong with her zat a soupçon of talent wouldn't cure. Zat will be all for today. In our next class we will rehearse your solo, Millicent. Let us hope you can dance ze Lilac Fairy as well as Willow.'

Willow and Danny swap secret looks. He dropped me on purpose.

I bolt out into a corridor squirming with leotards. When I reach my dorm, I jam a chair against the door and rush to the little bathroom. Cold water gushes from the tap. I swill out my mouth and spit out the blood.

What am I going to do? The lifts in *Swan Lake* are harder than anything I've practised before and if Danny drops me again, I could get injured. I need help.

Didn't the Captain say our mentors are supposed to guide and advise us? Filipp may not care about me, but I think he really does care about ballet. He might understand.

'Filipp, I need you.'

Filipp's face flickers in the bathroom mirror.

'What do you want?' He squints at my chin. 'You look terrible.'

'My dance partner dropped me – Filipp, what should I do? They want me to do these lifts, but I'm scared.'

'Then you must practise more – or are you scared of hard work too?'

'No, it's more than that. You know what it's like when everyone has such high expectations. We're actually quite alike, you and me. Your mum won a Scarlet Slipper. My mum won a Scarlet Slipper. I let mine down. You, well, you sort of let—' My words tumble to a stop.

'Are you daring to compare my family with yours? Your history with mine?' Filipp's cheeks turn blotchy. 'I am a POPOV! I have scarlet in my veins. Do you hear me? *Scarlet!* I am superior to you in every way. If the Debello boy dropped you, it was because you deserved to be dropped. You will never dance like a Popov. Never. Ever. Ever. Ev—'

Filipp's face vanishes as I rip off my Swanphone. Maybe Danny didn't drop me on purpose. Maybe my core was too weak. I don't need a mentor, I need my mum.

I watch the tears wriggle down my cheeks. *Mum. Where are you?*

There's only one thing to do. I run to my cupboard, pull on my hoody, reach for my beret and stuff what I can into my backpack.

I ignore the stares that follow me through the hall and out into the drizzle. No one comes after me. No alarm bells ring. Maybe they've realized they're better off without me.

As I splosh down the gravel drive, I regret not planning my escape better. Bab's in Buenos Aires and I'm on foot. Even if I knew where to go, I wouldn't know how to get there.

At that moment, there's a honk behind me. A dark-red van with *Meekes, Makers of Fine Dance Shoes* in olde-worldy gold letters slows down alongside me.

Pip winds down the window. 'Where are you going, miss? Do you need a lift?'

Rain trickles down my neck. I take one long last look at Swan House and jump into the van.

'Where to?' says Pip.

To the only person who might understand. 'To Meekes.'

13

The Homing Shoes

We slow past the gatehouse and pass through the gates.

'Is everything all right, miss?' asks Pip.

I shake my head. I can't tell Pip I'm running away without crying again.

As we zig-zag out of the park and into the traffic, I stare out of the window. Little ant people are pouring in and out of the Tube. They're huddling in doorways and sheltering in cafes. I wonder if Mum is one of them.

'You're awfully quiet, miss,' says Pip.

'Am I? Sorry.' I scrabble around for something to say. 'How long have you been working at Meekes, Pip?'

'Almost a year now. Started off unloading the vans, then Mrs H-P took a shine to me and I got my place on the bench. Just been promoted from soft toes to hard. Miss, I hope you don't mind me asking, but how did you get that bruise on your chin?'

'I fell,' I say. 'It was nothing.'

Pip shakes his head like I'm brave or something. 'You dancers are a tough lot.'

I glance at the steering wheel – at the blisters on his hands. 'So are you makers. Are your hands always sore?'

'You sort of get used to the pain after a while. Just as well, with everything that's happened at work this week. To be honest, some of us think we've got a ghost, you know, like one of those poltergeists. Diamond Maker swears he's heard moaning at night.'

'A *poltergeist*? Does Mr Stubbs think so too?'

'No, not Heart Maker. I keep telling him to look out, but he won't be told.'

We turn into a narrow back street and the van rattles over the cobbles.

'Here we are, miss. Back entrance.' Pip pulls into a parking bay and I jump out.

Outside, the clouds have puffed away and the sky is a pale September blue. I follow him through a small courtyard to the back of the building. We clang up a fire escape and straight into the shop, where Mrs Huntley-Palmer is sitting cross-legged on the carpet. The foot of a bored-looking girl rests in her hands. Mrs H-P smiles when she sees me, then frowns at my bruise.

'Are we finished Mrs H-P?' drawls the girl. 'I have a *Nutcracker* rehearsal at two.'

'All done.' Mrs Huntley-Palmer's frown follows me to the stairs.

Down in the basement, a couple of the makers are having a break over a bacon sandwich. 'Heard it again last night,' says one.

'If you ask me, it's the ghost of Edwina Meekes,' says the other. 'Fierce she was. Always said it'd take more than a coffin to carry her out of the place – do you remember, Alf?'

Mr Stubbs looks up from a wad of paper. 'Don't you start, Bert. This place is older and creakier than me and you put together. All this talk of moanin' and the like is tommyrot.'

He spots me behind Pip, but his eyes don't crinkle like they usually do when he sees me. ''Ello, Miss Millicent. Is somethin' the matter?'

I tuck my chin in my hoody. 'I wondered if I could ask you something. It's quite important.'

The makers put down their sandwiches to listen, but Mr Stubbs waves a sheet of paper. 'Make a start on this, will you, Pip? Five and an 'alf, she wants – 'essian – strong, with a bit of a taper. Come through to the kitchenette, miss. We can talk there.'

The kitchenette isn't a room exactly, more of a corner behind a rack of shoes. Mr Stubbs fills the kettle and takes a pint of milk from the fridge underneath the counter.

'Cup of Rosie, miss? Got a nice new kettle.'

'Yes please.'

'Still take it like your mum? Milk and 'alf a sugar?' I nod. 'What is it then, miss? Ask away.'

The words that come out aren't the ones I planned. 'Mr Stubbs. I've run away from school.'

Mr Stubbs nods like he knew all along. He pulls out a stool nestling under the counter. 'Sit yourself down and tell me all about it. I 'ope it ain't nothin' to do with that shiner on your chin.'

I pull off my beret, and it all comes out in a big sob. I tell him about Madame and having to dance all the leads. I tell him about Willow being so horrible and Danny dropping me. 'I can't stay at Swan House – I can't do it without Mum. I've got to find her. *Please,* Mr Stubbs, can you help me?'

Mr Stubbs's shaggy eyebrows meet in the middle. He pours hot water into a china teapot. 'I wish I could, miss, I really does, but the way I sees it is this – there's good people out there lookin' for 'er. Them that knows what they're doin'. They'll find 'er, miss, I'm sure of it. In the meantime, your mum'd want you to go back to school an' do your dancin'.'

'But Willow's turned everyone against me.'

'Not all of 'em, surely, miss. What about that nice young lady, Miss Lottie? She ain't the sort to listen to Miss Willow's nonsense. And the lad, Danny – 'e ain't a bad sort neither, just the type to be easily led. I admit, there ain't much you can do about Madame de La Cloche. Between you an' me an' the stage door, she's too huppity for her own good.'

'Huppity?'

'That's what I said. Anyway, if you asks me, it's Ms Celia's opinion what really matters. She'd never 'ave picked you to dance all them leads if she didn't believe in you. You got an opportunity, miss. A chance some would bite off your arm for.' Mr Stubbs's eyes twinkle. They're the same blue as the teapot and twice as shiny. 'All you got to do is find the pluck to take it.'

'But Mr Stubbs, I'm all out of pluck. I think my pluck is wherever Mum is.'

Mr Stubbs pats my hand. 'Wait there. I got somethin' for you. I was savin' them for the Scarlet Slippers but I reckon you need 'em now.' He leaves me puzzling and comes back with a shoebox. 'Open it, then.'

I pull off the lid. Inside is a pair of *pointe* shoes. When I lift them out, a tingle goes down to my toes. Next to the black hearts stamped on the soles are the initials 'E. L.'

Eva Lilova. They're Mum's.

I hold them to my heart.

'These are the first pair of shoes I made for your mum. She'd just started at the Royal Ballet and 'ad the biggest case of 'omesickness I ever saw. Ran away in 'em, she did.'

'Mum ran away?'

'That's right. But the next day I found her upstairs in the shop – she reckoned the shoes brought 'er back. I said they was like a pair of 'omin' pigeons my old dad kept in the war. We 'ad a laugh about that. She asked me to keep 'er 'omin' shoes for someone else who might need 'em. I 'ad a funny feelin' it might be you.'

'*Thank you*, Mr Stubbs!'

'Now – you could dance back to Swan 'ouse, miss, but I think it'd be quicker if I called Ms Celia, what do you say?'

14

0

Ms Celia zooms through the puddles. 'You and I have much to discuss. But first things first, why did you run off like that?'

I clutch the shoebox and wonder what spies do to children who run away.

'Well? Madame said you fell during a lift today.'

'I didn't fall, I was dropped, but it's more than that, Ms Celia, you don't understand.'

She steps on the accelerator and Winifred roars. 'You're right, Milly. And that is because I am not a mind reader. But I am a spy and I've done a little detective work. The Captain tells me that Tom Garrick fired an unauthorized weapon at you in the woods yesterday.'

'Yes, but it didn't hit me. He looked awful when we found him. Did he break his ankle?'

'Unfortunately, yes. He had to go straight to

hospital.'

Sunshine streams through the windscreen but I feel a sudden chill. 'H-he didn't say *I* did it, did he?'

Ms Celia lowers her sunshade. 'Quite the opposite. He told us you'd half carried him back to school.'

'Merv helped too.'

'You both behaved admirably, but the fact is, Milly, we can't have you running away again. You were invited here for a purpose.'

'I know. I have to make friends with one of Korolev's students.'

'That's right, but there's something else. You may have heard mention of someone called O?'

I grip the seatbelt as we swerve into the park. 'Topsy said he was your boss but no one ever sees him.'

'Emmeline is correct. O's identity is highly classified.'

We pass through the glade of spindly trees. I think back to my first day as the sunlight makes stripes on the tarmac. In, out, in, out. Only this time they make me think of prison bars.

Ms Celia pulls up outside the gates and the hairy hand waves her past the gatehouse. Moments later, Swan House comes into view and Winifred grinds to a noisy stop outside the porch.

I wonder why Ms Celia wants to talk about O.

Maybe it's O who deals with spies who run away?

When I ask her she shakes her head. 'Then what's O got to do with me?'

Ms Celia turns to look at me. Her eyes are as deep and dark as the lake. 'Everything.'

'What do you mean?'

'Milly, my dear, O is your mother.'

My hand slides from the seatbelt. 'No,' I say. 'NO. Mum can't be O. Her name begins with an *E* for Eva – *Eva Kydd*.'

Ms Celia reaches for my arm. 'Think, Milly. Which role made her famous?'

'*S-Swan Lake* . . . What's that got to do with anyth— Oh, *O*-dette and *O*-dile.'

'Exactly.'

'I don't believe it.'

'I'm afraid it's true. She was recruited to Swan House as a girl, just like you were. When she graduated, she went on to work for the school.'

'But she trained at the Royal Ballet School.'

'Only until her final year. Then she came here. Your grandmother didn't know, of course.'

My head begins to throb. 'So Mum's a *spy*?'

Ms Celia nods. 'One of the best – the head of our entire organization, in fact. And we think that's why she was taken.'

'*Taken*? Taken by who? Not . . .' The name sticks

to the roof of my mouth. 'Not Korolev?'

Ms Celia stares across the lake. 'We believe Korolev kidnapped her on the evening of the Scarlet Slippers.'

'But why?'

'Ivan and Eva were in Swan House together. It was Eva who caught him using poison the night before the Scarlet Slippers. He blamed her for his downfall. We think he means to win this year's competition at any cost. Possibly by using Eva as a bargaining chip.'

Thoughts stomp through my brain. Mum didn't leave because she wanted to. She didn't leave because I tripped Willow. It wasn't my fault, but isn't this worse? Mum has been kidnapped by a poisoner, and a cheat, and a Very Bad Man.

'So, you see, Milly, by staying to fulfil your part of the mission, you will be helping to rescue your mother.' Ms Celia's elbow catches the horn. We both jump. 'Sorry. How careless of me.'

Ms Celia is never careless. I suppose Mum's identity is a secret she'd rather have kept to herself. 'Ms Celia, does Willow Perkins know about Mum?'

'None of our students know O's identity, or even that O is missing. I will announce the purpose of the mission when I see fit. Until then, this information must remain top secret. Do you understand, Milly?

You mustn't say a word.'

When I tiptoe into the dorm that night, Willow's mouth drops open. 'I thought you'd gone,' she says.

'I've decided to stay for a bit longer, if it's all the same to you.'

Willow and Bumble start talking about me like I'm not here. But I've got another voice in my head. A voice that conjures up buttery toast and perfumed hugs.

Sorry, sweetheart, I have to go away for a couple of days. Just a short tour this time. I'll be back for your birthday . . .

Memories are springing up like daisies.

The time Mum was delayed in Paris because she missed her plane.

The time she was held up in Moscow because of the snow.

Missed planes. Bad weather. Mum is a spy. What else don't I know?

I jump into bed, tuck Mum's homing shoes under my pillow and hug Boris to me. If Mum needs rescuing, she needs someone brave and clever. Someone who cracks codes and karate kicks. Someone who isn't afraid of men with bluebottle-black hair and shifty eyes.

But more than that, she needs someone who can dance.

Cycni venustas – cor leonis.

She needs someone with the grace of a swan and the heart of a lion.

That someone is not going to be Willow Perkins. That someone is going to be me.

Eventually, Willow and Bumble doze off but I don't even try to sleep. In the end, I spend hours making shapes out of the clouds on the ceiling. I find a cat, a shoe, an O.

An O.

If Mum is a spy, wouldn't she have left clues? I tiptoe to my trunk and pull out her Scarlet Slippers programme. Once I'm in the bathroom, I run the light from my Swanphone over the cover and shine it on Mum's scribble.

YES.

If it means what I think it means, I just found Mum's first clue.

15

L'Odette

Spencer pulls up his hood. 'Remind me again, Kydd. Why have we swapped breakfast for a morning hike?'

'Yeah, and where are we goin'?' says Lottie. 'I ain't been this far into the woods before.'

Something rustles in the undergrowth. I look over my shoulder and swipe the rain from my eyes. 'I need to tell you something. Do you think anyone can hear us out here?'

'Doubt it,' says Lottie. 'But you never know wiv us being monitored non-stop and Merv bein' so paranoid. What is it, Milly?'

'Just a little bit further and I'll explain.'

Lottie flashes her Swanphone at my face. 'Flamin' Nora. What have you done to your chin?'

I blink. 'Nothing.' I've got more important things to worry about right now than Danny Debello. 'I fell in class yesterday – it was an accident.'

Lottie squelches after me. 'If someone's been givin' you a hard time, I'll have a word.'

'A "word"? Remind me, is that Mandarin, Malay or Cockney for a punch on the nose?' says Spencer.

Lottie ignores him. 'What is it, then, Milly? Any furver and we'll be up to our necks in flamin' duckweed. Listen!'

A familiar pitter-patter fills my ears. I clamber over the fallen tree and wait for them to catch up. 'It's OK, we're here.'

Lottie spots the boat first. There's a name peeling across its side. '*L'Odette*,' she reads. 'Like the White Swan.' She points at the hut. 'I never knew that was here neiver.'

'I found it when I was running away from Willow.'

'*I* found it first.' Spencer lowers his hood and runs his fingers through his hair. It sticks up in blond spikes before falling perfectly in place.

'Does it matter?' says Lottie. 'Let's get out of the rain.'

We pile inside the boathouse. Lottie plucks a slug off the rug and we plonk ourselves down.

'So,' says Spencer. 'What's the big secret? Better be worth missing scrambled brains for.'

My voice begins to quiver. 'It's Mum.'

Spencer yawns. 'What about her?'

Lottie kicks Spencer's foot. 'They ain't found her, have they?'

'Not exactly.'

'So, what is it then?'

I pause. Telling Lottie and Spencer will make it even more real. 'She's a spy.'

'Your *mum's* a bleedin' *spy*?'

Spencer's jaw drops. 'No way. That's so cool. My mother's an interior designer. Do you know how dull it is watching paint dry?'

'It's more than that, Spencer. Ms Celia told me Mum is O. She's Ms Celia's boss. She's everyone's boss!'

'You have got be jokin',' says Lottie.

'I wish I was. Ms Celia said that's why she was kidnapped. Our mission is to rescue her.'

A spider scuttles past Spencer's foot. '*Kidnapped?* This hasn't got anything to do with Ivan, has it?'

'Yes. Sorry, Spencer. He and Mum were at Swan House together. Ivan's got some kind of vendetta against her.'

'Flamin' Nora,' says Lottie again.

'Well, that's awkward,' says Spencer. 'My mentor kidnapping your mother and all.'

'Do you think he'd know something that might help us find her?'

'It's unlikely, but maybe I can get *something* out of the little weasel.' Spencer lifts his wrist. 'Ivan. Need to talk.'

Ivan Korolev appears and sits cross-legged next to Spencer. 'How can I help you, Benedict? Ahh, I know this place. I used to come here to – how to say in English? – "bunk off" Ethics in Espionage.' He smiles his half smile.

'Ivan, listen, did you know a girl called Eva Kydd when you were at school?'

'Eva Kydd? I'm sorry, I cannot help you. That is classified information.'

'Wait a minute, Spence,' I say. 'Kydd is Mum's married name, she was Eva *Lilova* at school.'

'Eva Lilova? Yes, of course, I remember her,' says Ivan. 'I partnered her many times. She vas a beautiful dancer.'

My throat goes scratchy. 'Do you remember arguing with Eva, after she caught you using poison at the Scarlet Slippers?'

'I'm sorry, I don't understand. Please repeat the qvestion.'

'At the competition, you argued—'

Ivan flickers. 'I am unable to process your reqvest.'

'Try rephrasing the question,' says Spencer. 'Ivan, did you ever argue with Eva Lilova?'

'No. Vhy vould I?'

'He's tellin' the truth,' says Lottie. 'Mentors can't lie. If he and Eva did fall out, it must have been after his hologram was made.'

'I did not argue vith Eva,' Ivan says, 'but Blanche did.'

'Blanche?' says Spencer. 'Do you mean *Madame*?'

'Yes, Blanche de La Cloche.'

'She was in school with Eva?'

'Vith Eva. Vith me. She vas as jealous of Eva as vinter is of summer.'

'Why?'

'It is obvious. Eva vas gifted. She'd vun a Scarlet Slipper.' Ivan sighs. 'It is every dancer's greatest vish to vin a Scarlet Slipper.'

'That explains why she's so horrible to you, Milly,' says Lottie. 'Madame's gettin' her own back on your mum.'

'Maybe,' says Spencer. 'But unfortunately, that means that Madame isn't going to help you, Kydd. Thanks, Ivan. You can scoot.' Ivan vanishes. 'Shame he changed sides. I quite like him.'

I pull the programme from my backpack. 'There's something else. It's Mum's programme from the Scarlet Slippers. Look what's inside.'

'Ha!' Lottie pokes the photograph. 'That's never you! You got hair!'

'Not the picture, Lottie. Look at the handwriting.'

'Let me see.' Spencer holds the programme up to the window. 'There's a pen mark. A letter? It might be an *M*?'

'You're looking at it upside down, Spencer.'

'Oh, right. Is it a *W*?'

'Yes, as in W for *Willow*?'

'No way. You fink Perkins has somefink to do wiv your mum's kidnappin'?'

'Maybe?' It does sound a bit mad when Lottie says it like that.

Spencer tucks the programme inside his hoody. 'I'll ask Mr Special to take a look. If he's so clever, he might be able to figure out what it means.'

When we get back, Topsy's waiting outside the dorm. 'Hellooo, Milly. I've been looking for you everywhere. I've got something for you from Tom Garrick. He left it at reception before he went to hospital. All hibbledy-hobbledy on crutches he was.'

I take a cautious peek inside the brown envelope. Tom is good friends with Willow. This might be some kind of practical joke.

I wait until Topsy's gone before sliding out a note. It's folded around a pretty gold compact and a packet of bobby pins.

Dear Milly, Nurse said if you hadn't helped me to the infirmary, things could have been much worse. I haven't got anything to give you except these – I 'borrowed' them from Madge and you might find them useful. Sorry I had you all wrong. Good luck at the Scarlet Slippers. Tom.

I show the note to Lottie. 'The compact is just like Bab's.'

'But why would Tom give you a thing of face powder?' says Spencer.

Lottie grins. 'It ain't any old compact – I fink it's a doobrie! Can't check it out here though. Could be fog powder. Or a show an' tell glass. Or a boomer-bang!'

Spencer snatches the compact. 'What's a boomer-bang?'

'A mirror that boomerbangs missiles back to where they came from.'

Blimey.

Our Swanphones hum. Lottie curses in Cockney. 'We're late for Madame. Tom's doobrie's goin' to have to wait.'

Spencer hands the compact back reluctantly. 'Just promise you won't open it without me.'

16

The Doobries

In Madame's class, something very odd is happening.

Dipti Patel smiles at me for the first time ever. Fleur Fontaine makes room for me on the barre. When I finish my bottle of water, Danny Debello offers me his.

What's wrong with everyone?

'Lottie,' I say at break. 'Have I got cabbage in my teeth?'

'No.'

'Anything stuck to my back?'

'Nah.'

'Holes in my tights . . . ?'

After break, I get to practise the *corps de ballet* dance with everyone else. Ms Celia gathers us around her. 'Now that you are all warmed up, we will begin rehearsing *Romeo and Juliet* for the competition.'

Spencer puts his hand up. 'Does that mean the boys get to use swords?'

Lottie stamps her foot. 'Why do the boys always get all the fun?'

'It's OK, Shorty,' says Spencer. 'You girls'll get little hankies to wave.'

Ms Celia frowns at Spencer. 'The boys may carry swords, but they will certainly not *use* them. Fencing lessons, for both boys *and* girls, are scheduled for next term.'

Lottie sticks out her tongue at Spencer.

'Now, can anyone tell me the story of *Romeo and Juliet*?'

'It's a love story, miss!' shouts Fleur.

'Yes. And what else?'

Lottie's hand shoots up. 'Romeo's a Montague and Juliet's a Capulet and the two families hate each other's guts. So there's a load of fightin'!'

'Thank you, Lottie. And then what happens?' Ms Celia sighs. 'Yes, Benedict?'

'Everyone dies . . . What? Did I leave something out?'

Dipti and Fleur giggle but Ms Celia is gazing out of the window. '*Romeo and Juliet* is a tale of love and hate, poison and death. The wonderful score, the powerful story, the beautiful choreography all come together to create –' she waves her hand like a magic wand – 'theatrical dark magic.'

There is total silence. Even Spencer's hooked.

'Now, I'd like you to get into character. Take a space on the floor. Imagine a grand ballroom . . . What is it Lottie?'

'I'm no good at imaginin' stuff, miss.'

'Well, think of our own refectory. It won't be long before it will be brought back to its former glory for the Scarlet Supper. Think how grand that will be.'

Lottie closes her eyes. 'Fanks, miss. I can see it now.'

'Try and imagine you are a *Capulet*. A member of the nobility. Feel the movement of your fine clothes. The weight of your headdress. Well done, everyone. Now listen to the music. It's called "The Dance of the Knights".'

The floor begins to vibrate. The beat goes through the soles of my feet, up through my calves and into the pit of my stomach. 'Weave around each other,' says Ms Celia. 'Slow and dignified . . . Lottie, is that dignified? When the music stops, acknowledge the lord or lady next to you with a nod or a curtsy, then strike a regal pose and hold it like a statue!'

I freeze with my nose regally in the air. My hands regally on my hips.

'Remind you of anyone, *Willow*?' says Dipti.

Willow's eyes flash at Dipti. Her nose goes pink.

By the time class has finished, Lottie is hopping up and down, whispering about fog powder and boomerbangs. I try to leave but I can't get past the queue of people being nice to me.

'Don't take any notice of Willow,' says Dipti.

'Sorry about your chin,' says Danny. 'You can trust me from now on, I promise.'

'I'm sorry too,' says Fleur. 'I felt so bad out in the woods. We should never have chased you like that.'

Danny nods. 'Yeah, when Tom fell, Willow was going on about the Dance of Death so we just left him there. He was lucky you came along.'

Lottie grabs my arm. 'LET'S GO!'

'One moment, everyone,' calls Ms Celia. 'The Captain wishes to see you before lunch. Please go straight to the gym.'

Spencer groans. 'I didn't have breakfast. I'm so hungry I could eat a hot-water bottle cat-thing.'

Ms Celia takes me aside. 'Milly – a brief word before you go. You did well today. I'm glad you weren't too upset by our conversation yesterday.'

Lottie follows us into the corridor. 'What about me, miss?'

'You were perfectly competent, Lottie, but I suspect that your mind was elsewhere.'

Lottie's eyes flick to my bag. 'Uhhh – I was just thinkin' about them Capulets and Montagues and why they started fightin' in the first place.'

'Have either of you seen the play?' asks Ms Celia.

'Seen the film, miss,' says Lottie. 'Didn't understand a flamin' word.'

'I don't think Shakespeare gave a reason for the feud. It may well have been over nothing. People can fall out over such trivial things.' She glances at Willow. 'But even the smallest spark can destroy a forest if it's left to burn . . .'

All through Spy Craft, the doobries burn holes in my bag.

'Hen's teeth, Kydd! You're away with the bliddy fairies again,' shouts the Captain. 'What did I say *dry cleaning* was?'

'Uhhh, is it the thing old people do with their delicates? Bab takes hers to Clapham High Street.'

'Give us strength. *Dry cleaning* has nothing to do with your granny's *delicates*, Kydd. It's a counter-surveillance technique employed to check if an agent is being tailed.'

I can speak five languages and I still have no idea what he's talking about.

'You of all people need to pay attention,' he says. 'You know *what*, and *who*, is at stake.'

I hang my bob in shame. *Mum*. He means Mum is at stake.

Danny Debello puts up his hand. 'Are you talking about the mission, Captain? Can you tell us why we're after Ivan Korolev now?'

'I can tell you this. Korolev has something we want. Some*one*, in fact. A VIP. The head of Swan House.'

'You mean there's someone above Ms Celia?' asks Danny. 'Who's that?'

'I can only give you a code name. O's identity is top secret for obvious reasons.'

I notice Lottie and Spencer are pretending to find their copies of *The Guide to Espionage* totally fascinating too.

After supper, everyone is still talking about the identity of the mysterious O. Lottie, Spencer and I bolt down our food then dash back through the courtyard and crouch behind the dorms.

'Open the compact first,' says Spencer.

Lottie peeps around the corner. 'Better be quick, Madame's on the prowl.'

'Are you sure this is safe to open, Lottie?'

'Only one way to find out, ain't there?'

I hold the compact at arm's length and inch it open. A bright white light floods the shadows.

'Let me see.' Spencer inspects the compact carefully, then snaps it shut. 'What a let down. It's just a torch.'

Lottie tears open the packet of bobby pins. 'Universal lock picks. Handy, but they ain't much use in school.'

'Is that all? A torch and some lock picks?' I try not to feel too disappointed. 'I suppose it was nice of Tom to give me anything.'

'Uh-oh,' says Lottie. 'We got company.'

A ghostly figure appears out of the gloom. 'Who is zere? Is zat you, Millicent Kydd?' I blink as Madame shines her Swanphone from my face to Lottie's. 'Charlotte Li,' she tuts. 'And who is zis?' Spencer's hair lights up like an angel's. 'Benedict Spencer? What are you all doing out here in zc dark?'

'I ain't feelin' too good,' says Lottie. 'Came over all funny after Cook's spotted dick – better get to the loos before I chuck again. *Bonne nuit*, Madame!'

'You are up to something, Charlotte Li.'

'Not *moi*, miss.'

'Well, in zat case you will not mind if I see you all to your dormitories.'

Back in the dorm, Willow is lying on her bed, ranting on about the way I've pulled the wool over everyone's eyes and how I'll suffer once they've learnt what I'm really like. In the bed next to her, Bumble nods along like a little nodding dog. I feel for Tom's letter in my pocket and for the first time, Willow and Bumble don't bother me one bit. In fact, Willow wears herself out in no time, and pretty soon they're both fast asleep. It's only when I get into bed I notice that Boris is missing.

That night, I dream of Willow falling from the Dance of Death.

17
Kristina the Knife

'*Ay-ya!*' Lottie deadheads the last of the pansies in the courtyard and a wake of dead petals swirls behind her. 'Take that! And that, sweetcheeks!'

I hang back while she looks around for something else to karate chop. Lottie's dangerous when she's bored.

'Did you find that cat-thing of yours?' shouts Spencer over the howling wind.

I shake my head. Two months have gone by since Tom Garrick left and I'm still hot-water bottle-less. Actually, it's the real Boris I'm worried about. It'll be November tomorrow and he hates fireworks. Boris pretends to be tough but he's really an old scaredy-cat. Where's he going to hide? I don't suppose the Bombardier's got a wardrobe full of fake fur.

I sigh. 'She won't admit it, but I'm sure Willow catnapped him.'

'I wish you'd let me have a word,' says Lottie.

'Thanks, Lottie but one of your "words" would only make things worse. I just wish I could sleep without him. I lie awake all night thinking I should be helping Mum right *now*, but every single second of the day is taken up with lessons.'

'If you think about it, the whole *point* of lessons is to help your mother,' says Spencer.

Lottie kicks through a pile of coppery leaves. 'But lessons ain't *action*, are they, Spence.'

Spencer puts his fingers to his lips. 'Quiet, Shorty. *POS*.'

'Uh?'

'*Perkins Over Shoulder . . .*'

'Hi, Milly,' says Willow. 'You were great in class this morning. I totally get why Ms Celia cast you to play the White Swan now.'

I do a Willow and roll my eyes. Surprisingly, everyone in school is still being nice to me. Not surprisingly, it's driving Willow around the twist, especially since she's started to pretend to like me too. Bottling up all that loathing can't be good for a person.

'It's your birthday tomorrow, isn't it?' she adds brightly. 'I don't suppose you'll get many presents with all your family gone and everything, but you know – birthdays aren't really about presents, are they? They're about *friends*.' Willow squeezes my arm.

I'd managed to push my birthday to the back of my mind until now. Trust Willow to bring it up. As she skips away, I remind myself to ask Merv about the 'W' Mum wrote in her programme. She was definitely trying to tell me something bad about Willow, but what?

'Like *she* knows anyfink about friends.' Lottie kicks another pile of leaves in the archway. This time the wind blows them back in her face.

'I'd save your energy if I were you,' says a muffled voice.

Lottie raises her fists. Her eyes slide from side to side.

Ms Celia's head appears from behind Winifred's bonnet. 'Did you hear me, Lottie? I wish you'd put as much effort into our dance rehearsals.' She slams the bonnet and slips a spanner into the pocket of her overalls.

'Oh, it's you, Ms Celia. I'm doin' my best, honest.'

'And Milly, it wouldn't hurt for you to put in some extra practice too. Hurry now, lunchtime is over.'

My shoulders slump. I'm working as hard as I can, but it's difficult to concentrate on anything with a kidnapped mother on your mind. I watch Ms Celia disappear inside one of the garages then turn to Spencer. 'You haven't seen Merv recently, have you?'

'No, I gave him your programme and haven't seen him since. He's stopped coming to Spy Craft and he must have found somewhere else to sleep.'

Lottie bats a leaf out of her hair. 'Merv might be in Petrenko's class this afternoon. Considerin' he's so clever, his Russian's rotten. You're so lucky you don't have to do Russian, Milly. Who've you got instead?'

'For some reason, I've got to meet Madge in wardrobe.'

'That'll be for a fittin',' says Lottie.

'Madge makes costumes too?'

'You could say that.'

I spot Dafydd Wynn-Jones perched on a table heaped with little boxes of buttons and beads. 'Hi, Milly. Getting your costumes made?'

Dafydd's eyes remind me of Boris. I nod, and wish my cheeks would behave.

'Great. I think clothes can really help you to feel the part.'

'I hope so. I need all the help I can get.'

He smiles. 'Works for me. That and a lot of practice! Keep trying and you'll get there.'

'Thanks, Dafydd.'

Madge Little scurries in wearing a white lab coat over her nightie. 'Are you both here for a fitting?' She pulls on a huge pair of goggles.

'No,' says Dafydd. 'You're making my hologram, remember?'

'Am I? Oh yes. With the Scarlet Slippers coming up, I don't know if I'm coming or going. Give me a moment and I'll reprogram the scannaray.'

The *scannaray*? Madge disappears behind a moving rail of sparkly costumes.

'Going to be a mentor next year,' says Dafydd. 'My Swanphone's already given them most of my data. One more scan and I'll be done.'

I envy the lucky year seven who's paired with Dafydd.

Ten minutes later, it's my turn. I step into a little photobooth in my vest and tights. Madge tells me to close my eyes – apparently I'm about to be 'scan-narayed'. There's a humming sound and a bright flash which goes right through my eyelids. It's very discombobulating.

'All done,' says Madge. 'The 4D Printonic will produce your headdresses, tutus, masks, everything you need. They'll be ready by teatime.'

Wow.

My Swanphone glows. 'Mr Crump wishes to see you next.'

I ask who Mr Crump is and my Swanphone goes all mysterious. 'Your mentor will take you to him.'

I sigh. I haven't seen Filipp since I ran away and I wouldn't mind if I never saw him again. When he appears, he's wearing the same expression as Bab when she sucks on a sherbet lemon.

'What do *you* want?' I have to remind myself that he's only a hologram.

'Do you know where Mr Crump is?'

'Of course. He's where he always is. In the control room above the theatre.'

'You mean that little room where all the sound and lighting stuff is?'

'Yes. *That* little room. It's this way.'

I grab my bag and follow Filipp up the stairs. Across the landing, muffled shouts escape the gym. Invisible lasers sweep the corridor.

Filipp's see-through shoulders are slumpier than mine. I try to ignore the little twang inside me but it's impossible not to feel sorry for someone who trips over their own feet every five minutes.

I decide to cheer him up.

'Filipp, I saw your mum's Scarlet Slipper in

Madame's trophy cabinet the other day.'

He hesitates, then carries on plodding. 'That's nothing. We have a trophy *room* at home.'

I picture Mum's Scarlet Slipper on the mantlepiece. If she had a whole *room* of trophies, I think I'd burst with pride. I suppose that's why Filipp always seems so – I search for the word – *huppity*.

'By the time I leave Swan House, our trophy room will contain *my* Scarlet Slipper too.' He trips outside a door I hadn't noticed before and the twang turns into a pang. Poor Filipp Popov. I wonder what became of him.

The first thing I see in the control room is a console glinting with knobs and buttons. The second is a bank of computer screens. The third is a shock of bushy black hair and a pair of panda-rimmed eyes. Merv looks like he hasn't slept for days. Then I catch a reflection of the ghost of a panda in the glass. Neither do I.

'Hi, Merv. I thought Mr Crump would be here.'

Merv spins his chair to face me. 'He is.'

I look up. Down. Under the console.

'You're looking at him.'

'*You're* Mr Crump?' I throw down my bag and

swivel a chair under the console. Stacked in the corner is a tower of sandwich boxes.

'Did I say you could sit?'

I stand up and knock over a *Star Trek* thermos.

Merv twitches. 'OK, sit down! Just don't touch anything.'

The control room looks over the theatre. Onstage, Dafydd has joined Madame and Willow for a rehearsal. 'Can they see me up here?'

'No. All of the windows in Swan House are shatter-, bullet- and snoop-proof.'

Merv turns one of the dials on the console. The house lights dim. As the spotlight follows Willow and Dafydd, music floats up from the theatre. They're so much better than me and Danny. For the hundredth time, I wonder why Ms Celia chose me to dance the principal roles.

'Why did you need to see me, Merv?'

Merv roots around in his satchel and hands me a folder. 'Ms Celia asked me to give you something – it's Level RLB so don't leave it lying around.'

'RLB?'

'*Read me. Learn me. Burn me.* Actually, you might want to just give it back to me when you've finished. The last person to use the incinerator in the basement lost their eyebrows.'

I swivel in the chair. 'What is it?'

'Can you please keep still?'

'Sorry.'

'It's your mission.'

I stop swivelling.

Over the past couple of months, I've got used to switching from *jetés* to judo in less time than it takes to change my footwear, but I'm SO not ready for anything that could be described as a *mission*.

A photograph slips out of the folder. The girl in the picture has blonde plaits, rosy cheeks and ruby lips. 'Is she the Casovan girl I've got to make friends with?'

'Her name is Kristina Kovalchuk,' says Merv. 'Known in the trade as *Kristina the Knife*. She approached us a couple of months ago wanting to sell information. We think she wants to talk about your mum. That's where you come in.'

'Wait a sec. You knew my mum had been kidnapped AND DIDN'T TELL ME?'

'There's no need to shout. I only found out this morning.'

'DID YOU KNOW MUM WAS O?'

'Stop shouting! I had my suspicions, but until now, O's identity has been top secret.' Merv blinks. 'Can I finish now?'

'OK. Sorry about the shouting.'

'Kristina will only speak to someone she trusts.

You speak her language, plus you're Eva's daughter. She knows you won't double-cross her.'

'She looks quite nice.'

'Don't be fooled by her looks. They don't call her Kristina the Knife for nothing. The file tells you everything you need to know. Remember, it's FYEO.'

'Uh?'

'*For Your Eyes Only*. Read it ASAP – *As Soon As Possible*, then bring it back.' Merv spins back to the console. 'TAFN – *That's All For Now*.'

I pause at the door. 'Merv, did you get a chance to look at Mum's programme?'

'No. I'm very busy.' Merv lowers his voice. 'But that reminds me, before you decide to go sneaking into the woods again, you might want to turn off your Swanphone. You don't know who's watching.'

My face burns. 'You haven't told anyone, have you?'

'Not yet.'

'Thanks, Merv. Ooo, and I don't suppose you saw anyone take Boris, did you?'

Merv's fingers hover over his keyboard. 'Who's Boris?'

'My hot-water bottle. Fat. Ginger. Looks like a cat?'

'When?'

'A couple of months ago.'

Merv looks at me sideways. 'We're having teething troubles with the new security system. There's been a glitch with the cameras. But don't tell anyone. It wasn't my fault.'

'I didn't say it was. I just want to find Boris.'

'Sorry. Can't help. Just read the file and bring it back first thing. FYEO, remember?'

'OK, but can't I just read it here?' I swing my arm and clip Merv's sandwich-box tower. One by one they clatter onto the console.

'No.' Merv removes the one on his lap. 'And Kydd – remind me never to ask you up here again.'

FYEO? Huh. That's easier said than done in school full of spies.

Where am I suppose to go? The dance studios are busy. Bumble's in the dorm. Cook's in the refectory. Topsy's *omm*ing in the yoga studio. It's too rainy to sit outside. Too late to trek to my boathouse. I peep in every room I'm allowed to peep in before heading back to the theatre.

The rehearsal has finished and the theatre is still and peaceful – like a sort of *Sleeping Beauty*. I walk down the aisle and climb the steps to the stage. There's a stool in the wings so I sit myself down and pull Kristina Kovalchuk's file from my bag.

I study her picture. She doesn't look like a 'crim' to me.

According to the file, Kristina loves ballet, hates books and is allergic to bouncy castles. Her hobbies are knitting and knife-throwing.

There are more pictures in the folder. One's of a dancing Kristina. One's of a knife-throwing Kristina. The little boy handcuffed to the wall looks petrified.

I'm about to turn the page when the doors to the theatre swing open. I shuffle everything back inside the folder.

Footsteps pad along the aisle. The doors creak again and someone else comes in. I hold my breath. The theatre trembles as the Captain marches up to the stage steps.

'As I was saying,' says Madame, 'ze theatre needs to be fully secure before ze Scarlet Slippers come to Swan House.'

'Adaptations are underway,' says the Captain. 'The Crump boy has been tasked with upgrading the surveillance tech.'

'In the classrooms too?'

'Aye. Every inch of the school will have eyes and ears. Korolev won't be able to *promenade* without us knowing about it.'

The door opens again. 'Blanche – a word, if I may?' It's Ms Celia.

'Of course. We were just discussing ze work to ze theatre – do you have something to add?'

'No. I completely trust Garth's expertise,' says Ms Celia.

'Thank you, Celia. Actually, now that we're all here, there's something I'd like to say.' The Captain lowers his voice. 'It's about the mole.'

'What about the mole?' says Madame.

'I still have doubts.'

'Doubts? You *still* think we are mistaken? Zat is *ridicule*!'

The Captain tugs on his beard. 'The whole thing's bliddy daft, if you ask us. We've jumped to too many conclusions.'

Ms Celia glances at Madame. 'I understand why you might have concerns, Garth, but Blanche agrees that all the evidence points in one direction. There's no turning back now.'

The Captain heaves a sigh and three pairs of footsteps leave the theatre.

I wait until the doors have clunked shut and breathe out.

A mole? In Swan House? I don't suppose they mean a small, velvety creature who lives underground.

But that's Ms Celia's problem. I slide Kristina the Knife's file into my bag. I think I've got quite enough to worry about.

18

The Birthday Surprise

I tug my duvet over my ears but it's no good, I can't go back to sleep. There's a voice in my head, a velvety voice conjuring up cupcakes and candles.

Happy birthday, sweetheart. Close your eyes and make a wish . . .

I can't believe I'm a teenager.

Thirteen. And Mum's not here.

And nor is Bab.

And nor is Boris.

And when I tried to tell Lottie about the mole yesterday, she'd disappeared too.

It's my birthday, and I'M ALL ALONE . . .

I sob into my pillow then wipe my cheeks on the sheet. Feeling sorry for myself isn't going to get Mum back, is it?

There's a muffled *rat-tat-tat* on the door. I glance

across the dorm; Willow is making snuffly hamster noises and Bumble is snoring louder than the nine fifteen to Paddington.

'It's us,' whispers a voice outside.

'Open up, Kydd,' says another voice. 'It's *brrrr*uddy freezing out here.'

I yelp as the wind catches the door. Clouds race across the blue-black sky – a wisp of lilac sits on the rooftops.

Lottie and Spencer are both stamping their feet to keep warm.

'What are you doing? It's still night-time.'

Spencer yawns. 'Shorty woke me up at stupid o'clock. You'd think it was someone's birthday or something.'

Lottie grins. 'Happy birfday, Milly! Come on, we've got somefink to show you.'

'You have? What is it?'

'You'll have to wait and see! Get dressed. Quick!'

I pull on my clothes, grab the compact and close the door as quietly as I can. Behind the stables, the treetops are dancing wildly against the sky.

'Turn off your Swanphones,' I say. 'We can use the light from the doobrie.'

Spencer jogs ahead with the little gold compact. Lottie waits for me to pull my beret over my ears, then we follow the wavering light into the woods.

Once we're out of earshot, I raise my voice over all the moaning and creaking and tell them about Kristina the Knife and the conversation I overheard in the theatre.

'Are you sure they said *mole*?' says Spencer.

'Yes, and they know who it is.'

'So, who is it?' asks Lottie.

'They didn't say a name.'

'Could be anyone, couldn't it?' Spencer shines the compact at the fork in the path. 'It could be one of us . . .'

I think back to the W in Mum's programme. Is that what Mum was trying to tell me? Could Willow be the mole?

'Merv might know somefink?' says Lottie.

'I saw him shuffling up the stairs yesterday. He was doing this . . .' Spencer does a swivelly thing with his eyes. 'Looked very suspicious. Maybe the Merv has turned?'

Lottie snorts. 'You don't really fink Merv's a mole?'

Spencer shrugs. 'It's always the people you don't suspect. And how well do we really know Merv?'

'It can't be Merv,' I say. 'He's got a *Star Trek* thermos.'

'Well, he's hiding *something*,' says Spencer. 'The question is, what? Careful, Kydd. Brambles.'

Spencer holds back a prickly branch and I duck under his arm. 'I wish I could get Filipp to talk,' I say. 'He knows everything about the school.'

'He *finks* he knows everyfink,' says Lottie. 'And he don't half drone on—'

'Whoa.' Spencer stops dead. 'Look!' He holds out his hand. The little gold compact is vibrating. 'Shhh, listen!' Something is whirring inside.

Spencer's eyes widen as the compact flips in his hand. Four metal arms unfold from the case, each with a tiny propeller. 'Li, what did you say just now?'

We watch in amazement as the compact hovers above Spencer's outstretched palm.

'Uhh, we were talking about Filipp,' I say.

'Yeah – I said he don't half go on.'

Spencer grins. 'No you didn't! You said "*drone* on"! The doobrie's a drone! Well done, Li. You just voice-activated it!'

Wow.

'Drone – to the lake!' orders Spencer. The compact shoots off and we all run after it. Mist swirls around our feet as it hangs at the water's edge. Squiggles of light shimmy on the surface.

Spencer shakes his head. 'Who would have thought it? Madge Little's a genius.'

'Can we forget about Madge for a minute,' says Lottie. 'Close your eyes, Milly . . .' She guides me up the slippery bank. '. . . OK. You can open them now! HAPPY BIRFDAY!'

The boathouse is twinkling with fairy lights.

Spencer grins at my mouth making wow shapes. 'What is it with girls and fairy lights?'

'I love it! Thanks, both of you.'

'It was all Shorty's idea. Nothing to do with me,' says Spencer.

'Go on, Milly, look inside.'

I gaze up at the lights glowing from the rafters. Bobbing between them are dozens of balloons.

Spencer heaves a bag from his shoulder and dumps some parcels on the rug. 'Topsy gave us your post. These are all for you, birthday girl.'

'But you got to open our presents first.' Lottie passes me a huge bag of sweets. 'Lucky Candy – my dad brought them back from Singapore. Sorry, there wasn't much point in wrappin' them up, seein' as Spencer'd already EATEN HALF OF THEM.' She punches Spencer on the arm.

'*Ouch*! Blame Cook. I can't help it if I'm always starving. Anyway, I've more than made up for it.'

Spencer delves into his backpack and pulls out a paper take-out bag. A smell that makes my taste buds tingle fills the boathouse.

He dishes out burgers, chips and milkshakes. 'It's amazing what money and influence can buy.'

No one speaks for some time. Spencer eats without chewing and Lottie throws herself down on the rug. 'Does anyone else feel like chuckin' up? I ate that way too fast.'

Spencer looks at her like she's just asked him if he sings opera – or if he could live without his phone. 'I'm thirteen. I'm a boy. I can eat fast food until it comes out of my nose.'

I lick my fingers. 'I feel sick too, but in a good way.'

'You're both lightweightsh,' says Spencer with his mouth full. 'Anyway, Kydd, *thish* ish your proper preshent. My mother choshe it. She'sh good at preshentsh.'

'It's from Merv too,' says Lottie.

Spencer chokes on a chip. 'Merv's contribution was nine measly pence and a *Star Trek* sticker. Anyway, Kydd, go on, open it.'

I rip off the glittery paper and hold up an engraved silver box. I open it slowly and music tinkles out. A ballerina twirls inside. It's one of the best presents I've ever had.

'It's got a key so it's one hundred per cent Bumble and Perkins-proof,' says Spencer. '*I* wanted to get you a proper safe, like my father's. But I was overruled.'

'It's perfect! It's *all* perfect!'

Spencer unwraps one of Lottie's sweets. 'So, what

else have you got?'

I read out Bab's card first.

'*Happy thirteenth birthday, darling. Have the most wonderful day. Don't mind miserable old Madame, now you're a teenager you can break the rules and have fun!*

Much love, your Babushka.

PS. I hope you like my gift. I look forward to seeing you wearing it soon.

PPS. Alejandro says feliz cumpleaños!'

I show Lottie the silver charm. A small but perfect ballerina. My eyes are impossibly watery. 'It's just like the one Mum lost,' I explain.

'Has Madame still got your bracelet?' says Lottie. 'You should ask for it back. It *is* your birfday, ain't it.'

Spencer yawns. 'Better hurry up and open the rest. Haven't got a clue what the time is without my Swanphone.'

The Bombardier has sent me a book, *The Beginner's Guide to Fly-fishing*. *Hear you're next to a lake, old gal*, says the card.

'Is he an elephant short of a circus?' asks Lottie.

Spencer blows on his hands. 'We could always burn it. I'm frozen.'

I grab it back. 'I think it's very sweet of the Bombardier to remember.'

'Well, let's hope this isn't a pipe and slippers.'

Spencer passes me a large parcel wrapped in lots of brown paper and tied with old-fashioned string. My hands shake a little as I tear away the layers. Deep down I know it can't be from Mum, but still . . .

'That's more like it, 'cept it looks like an Easter egg and it ain't Easter,' says Lottie.

'It's better than an Easter egg.' I hold up the box so Lottie can see inside. 'Look, it's a white chocolate ballet shoe.'

'Who's it from, Milly?' asks Lottie.

I search the pretty gold packaging for a message. 'I don't know. I can't find a label.'

'Never mind the label,' says Spencer. 'When are we going to eat it?'

'Later. I'm stuffed.'

'Me too.' Lottie springs up. 'Time to get back. I could do wiv a warm-up.'

When I get back to the dorm, I pop the silver charm and Madge's doobries in my music box, and slide it under my bed.

I'm still wondering where to hide the chocolate ballet shoe when Madame's head bobs past the window.

My bracelet! I throw the box down. It slides off

the bed as I shoot outside.

'Madame, wait!'

A gust of wind blows off Madame's fur-lined hood. 'I am on my way out, Millicent. What do you want?'

Her eyes narrow as I explain about Bab's birthday present and ask for my bracelet. 'If I promise not to wear it, please can I have it back?'

'Zat will not be possible. Rules are rules. Zey apply to everyone, even Eva Kydd's daughter. I will make sure it is returned to you at ze end of term.'

'She wouldn't give it to you?' says Lottie at lunchtime.

'I'll speak to my father,' says Spencer. 'See if he can give her a heart transplant.'

'Ain't you got to have one in the first place? Eurgh!' Lottie glugs down her water then glugs down mine. She pokes out her tongue and wipes it on her napkin. 'Salt in the custard.'

Behind Lottie, Danny clears his throat and a little crowd gathers alongside him. 'Sorry to interrupt. We heard it was your birthday, Milly. So, we clubbed together and got you this.'

Danny gives me a parcel. 'Excuse the wrapping,' says Fleur. 'Danny needs practice.'

Dangling out of the paper is a little golden tail. I

tear off the tape. Inside is a hot-water bottle lion with golden fur and a fluffy mane.

Danny grins. 'It's not Boris, but it's the closest we could find.'

For the second time today, I'm lost for words. 'Thanks, everyone.'

'Happy birthday,' says Danny. 'See you in Spy Craft.'

'I hope the Captain doesn't spring anuvver test on us,' says Lottie, as we climb the stairs to the gym. 'I got two out of ten in Effics last week. What did you get, Spencer?'

'A very solid one,' says Spencer. 'Ethics are overrated, if you ask me. But you can ask me anything from the *Guide to Espionage*. It's Ivan's favourite book.'

'Anyfink? OK, what's Rule Eleven?'

'Never discount the obvious.'

'Rule Twelve?'

'When you've discounted the obvious. Look again.'

'Rule Nineteen?'

'Panic is the enemy of reason.'

Lottie shrugs. 'Swot.'

'The Captain can give me all the tests he likes today,' I say. 'I don't care.'

And I really don't. I thought my thirteenth was

going to be a birthday I'd want to forget, but thanks to my friends it's turning into one I'll always remember.

Lottie points at the gym. 'What's goin' on?' We pause as everyone piles onto the landing.

Spencer grins. 'Happy birthday, Kydd. Looks like Spy Craft's been cancelled.'

Lottie tugs my sleeve. 'Wait a minute. Am I seein' fings or is Perkins *cryin'*?'

Willow doesn't notice me as she pushes past. I get a horrible prickly feeling. Something is terribly wrong.

Dipti and Fleur run towards us.

'Oi! Where's everyone goin'?' shouts Lottie.

'Emergency assembly,' pants Dipti.

I ignore the flashing on my wrist. 'Why? What's happened?'

'Haven't you heard?' says Fleur.

'Heard what?'

'It's Bumble. She's been – she's been . . .'

'Spit it out,' says Spencer. 'She's been what? Good? Bad? To see the queen?

Dipti and Fleur both take breaths. '*Poisoned!*'

The noise in the theatre is deafening. Ms Celia is waiting onstage. Her forehead is busy thinking.

'There's Merv,' I say. 'He might know what happened.'

We wriggle through the children huddled in the aisles and plonk down next to Merv. My Swanphone flashes again. His eyebrow is busy worrying.

'Haven't you checked your messages?'

'Quieten down, please!' says Ms Celia. 'It seems most of you are already aware that one of our year eights has been taken gravely ill . . .'

'Kydd!' says Merv. 'Your Swanphone!'

'SHHH. This is an emergency, Merv.'

Merv makes a funny little whining sound.

'OK, OK.' I glance at my Swanphone. The Captain has sent me a video message. His expression is stormy.

'*Kydd. Please report to the infirmary immediately.*'

There's another.

'*Kydd, stop whatever it is you're doing and report to the infirmary NOW.*'

And another.

'*Kydd, if you're not dead already, you will be if you don't show up in the next five seconds.*'

Uh-oh. 'I'd better go to the infirmary.'

'Told you,' says Merv.

'About time,' says the Captain when I push through

the door. He takes me by the arm.

'Ouch! What's happening? Is Amy here? Is she going to be all right?'

'She's alive. For now.' The Captain sits me down. 'Wait there and don't move.' Seconds later, he comes back with Nurse.

'How are you feeling, Milly?' she says, sticking a thermometer on my tongue before I can answer. 'Okey-dokey, I'm just going to take your pulse. Any nausea?'

I shake my head as she takes out the thermometer.

'Well?' says the Captain.

'All normal. The readings on her Swanphone were correct.'

The Captain heaves a sigh. 'Thank God. Kydd, do you recognize this?' He shows me a picture on his Swanphone. Pieces of broken white chocolate are scattered across Bumble's bed.

'Y-yes. It was one of my birthday presents. I was saving it for later.'

'Did you take it out of the packaging? Did you see anyone eat it?'

'N-no. It was still in the box when I left it in my room. We'd had lots to eat, you see, and . . .' Suddenly, I realize what this means. 'Amy ate my chocolate?'

The Captain nods.

'And the chocolate was poisoned?'

'Aye. Korolev is back to his old tricks again. You do see what that means, pet?'

My scalp prickles. The poison was meant for me.

19

The Ghost of Edwina Meekes

I'm still in bed when the Captain messages me the next morning with a summons to meet him in the infirmary. Lottie springs up and rubs her eyes. The Captain overruled Madame and agreed that she could sleep in Bumble's bed last night. It's reassuring to know that if someone wants to hurt me, they'll have to get past Lottie first.

Willow moans, 'Is Bumble dead?'

I feel all woozy thinking about it. 'He – he didn't say. Sorry, Willow, I've got to go.'

Lottie leads the way. 'Wait here,' she says as we approach the archway. She throws herself against the wall, looks side to side, up and down, and beckons me through. 'Wait! Don't look now. Behind you. Ten o'clock.' Lottie crouches, ready to pounce.

'It's OK,' I whisper behind her. 'It's only Danny.'

Danny's face is as pale as Merv's. 'Have you heard

any news about Bumble?'

I shake my head. 'I'm going to the infirmary now. I'll let you know.'

When we arrive, the Captain thanks Lottie and sends her away. 'Come in, Kydd. We need to talk.'

I look through the window into the ward. The row of single beds is neatly made. There's not one Bumble-shaped lump under the blankets. My knees decide to take a little nap.

The Captain holds my arm. 'Sit down, pet. You're as white as the walls. Deep breaths, there's a good lass. It's all right. Ms Celia's antidote worked. Amy's gone home. She's still weak, but with a bit of rest she'll be dancing again before you know it.'

Footsteps pad behind me. 'Amy will miss ze Scarlet Slippers?'

'Yes, Madame. Nurse says she'll be back next term.'

'Zat is unfortunate.'

I sit up slowly. 'Can I go now?'

'Not yet, Millicent.' Madame glares at the Captain. 'You have not told her, Captain?'

'Told me what?'

The Captain pulls on his beard. 'Madge has given us the lab results from your birthday present. The chocolate wasn't from Korolev.'

My neck tingles. 'So, who was it from?'

'The parcel was an inside job.'

'I don't understand.'

Madame perches on the chair next to me and pats my arm. I squirm under her cold fingers. 'Ze parcel, it was not posted. It was from someone inside ze school.'

I shrink into the chair.

Someone in school hates me enough to want to poison me.

The obvious suspect is Willow Perkins but deep down I know Willow isn't a murderer. Plus, she'd know she was being monitored continually. Whoever left the package took a huge risk. 'Captain, if someone left it in reception, wouldn't they have been caught on camera? Wouldn't Merv have seen them?'

'No such luck, pet. There's been a problem with some of the security cameras.'

Madame's nails dig into my arm. 'I am sorry, Millicent. But zere are questions zat must be asked.' Her voice is snow-soft. Snow-cold. 'Ze chocolate was found on Amy's bed. Do you remember leaving it zere?'

'I-I didn't leave it on her bed, Madame. At least, I don't think I did. I saw you through the window and threw it down. Amy must have picked it up from the floor.' I wriggle my arm away and rub the half-moons Madame's nails have made in my skin.

The Captain nods. 'Aye, that's feasible enough.'

Madame stiffens. 'Are you sure, Captain? Ze

chocolate may have been intended for someone else all along. How do we know zat Millicent did not herself leave it on Amy's bed?'

'What do you mean? You think I wanted to poison Amy?' My voice is all screechy. In fact, the screechier it gets, the better I feel. 'You think I sent the chocolate to *myself*? This is about Mum, isn't it? You were jealous of her and you're taking it out on *me*!'

'Shhh, pet. There's no point in making things worse for yourself.'

Madame holds up her hand. 'I will handle zis, Captain. Millicent knows all about *jealousy*, don't you, *ma chère*? It is not *Amy* you wished to poison. Your jealousy of Willow is well known. Have you not tried to injure her in ze past? Perhaps you decided to take things a step further . . .'

I jump up. 'NO! No, I would never do anything like that!'

The Captain looks past me. 'Nurse, what does her Swanphone say?'

Nurse is sitting quietly in the corner. 'The readings indicate that she's telling the truth.'

Madame pahs. 'Remember, Captain, ze Swanphone is not foolproof when it comes to ze detection of lies.' Her Swanphone glows and she frowns at her wrist. 'I will let ze matter go – for now. Zere is a delivery I must see to.'

Nurse sees Madame out and the Captain lays a heavy hand on my shoulder. 'Kydd, promise us you won't say anything to anyone until we've got to the bottom of this.'

I shake my head. If Willow hears about it, I may as well pack my bags and leave.

'Good lass. You can go for breakfast now.' The kindness in his voice is like a squirt of de-icer on a frosty windscreen. 'But please be vigilant. As far as *I'm* concerned, you're still in danger.'

I trudge back to find Lottie but she's not in the refectory. In the hall, I spot Pip from Meekes.

'Hello, miss.' Pip's voice is as wobbly as the tower of shoeboxes in his arms.

I run over to help. 'Is there something wrong, Pip?'

Pip stacks the boxes next to the reception desk and pulls a tissue from the pocket of his overall. 'Sorry to be the one to pass on the bad news, Miss. But Heart Maker's had an accident. I told him those stairs were dangerous.'

The air whooshes out of me like a whoopee cushion without a whoop. 'I'll go and see him. Is he in hospital?'

Pip nods miserably and his fringe flops into his

eyes. 'Everyone's saying Edwina Meekes did it, miss.'

'You mean the *poltergeist*?'

He stares at his shoes. 'We're all wondering who's going to be next.'

I spot Madame crossing the hall towards us and my hands squeeze into fists.

'Madame, Heart Maker's in hospital. I have to go and see him.'

'He's in intensive care,' Pip explains. 'They don't know if he'll pull through. Mrs H-P's beside herself. We all are.'

Madame's face turns from white to grey. 'You think after everything zat has happened, you will be allowed to leave ze school? You will go to class immediately. And *you*,' she says to Pip, 'will return to Meekes.'

She shoos Pip from the hall but he calls out from the door. 'Miss Millicent – I almost forgot. Heart Maker gave me a message before they took him away.' His shoulders begin to shake. 'Said to keep wearing your m-mum's homing shoes. S-said you'd know what he meant. S-said you'd *got* to keep dancing.'

I slump in the corner. Pull on my flats. Go to the

barre. Stare at the floor. Poor Mr Stubbs.

When Madame comes in and says, '*Bonjours*, *les enfants*,' I don't reply.

When Lottie asks if I'm OK, I say I'm tickety-boo.

When the warm-up begins, my arms and legs are too heavy to move.

First Bumble and now Mr Stubbs. They can't die. They can't.

20

Merv's MUMB

December brings icy weather and more bad news. Mr Stubbs is getting worse.

And the poisoner is still at large.

Thanks to the Captain, Madame has kept her theory about the poisoned chocolate to herself. With just a week to go until the schools arrive for the Scarlet Slippers, my only comfort is the thought that I might see Mum again soon.

I haven't even been able to tell Lottie and Spencer about the chocolate. After the poisoning, the Captain ordered Filipp to EKAT – *Escort Kydd at All Times*. It's impossible to do anything you've been told not to do with a huppity mentor at your side from dawn till dusk.

'What's up, Milly?' says Lottie as we enter the refectory. 'Spencer finks you've been actin' strange lately.'

Using only my eyebrows, I try to explain that I can't talk in front of Filipp.

'Told you,' says Spencer. 'She's got that look on her face again, and she hasn't said a word in over a minute. That's not normal . . .'

Spencer's voice is drowned by a boo. Before I know it, I'm wiping a squashed satsuma from my forehead, and listening to laughter hoot from table to table.

'What's goin' on?' says Lottie.

'Ask Milly!' shouts Danny. 'Ask her who posted the chocolate that almost killed Bumble.'

Spencer steers us to a table as far away from Willow and her friends as possible. 'OK, Kydd. Time to spill.'

I explain about my so-called birthday present. 'Sorry, the Captain made me swear not to tell you. But now everyone's found out, they obviously think I left the chocolate out for Amy and Willow on purpose!'

Lottie makes a sound like a lion.

'Whoa . . .' Spencer grabs her hood. 'Not so fast, Shorty. Even you can't take on half the year. And if you look on the bright side, at least Kydd's had one of her five a day.'

Lottie bangs her fist on the table. 'Perkins is the poison around here. She's the one who left the chocolate on Bumble's bed. Her friends'll believe anyfink.'

Filipp gives me a sly smile. 'You're cleverer than you look.'

'Shut up, Filipp,' we all say together.

I push back my chair. 'I can't stay here.'

'Well, wherever you're goin', I'm comin' wiv you,' says Lottie. 'Where *are* you goin'?'

'To the kitchen, to research poison.'

Seems like the most obvious place to start.

As it turns out, Cook is quite the expert.

'They used arsenic in the old days,' she shudders. 'That old devil, Korolev, used Alpha X. It's not fatal but it plays havoc with your waterworks.'

I ask her how she knows so much. Cook squints at Filipp through the steam, then back at me again. 'It's supposed to be a secret, but you won't tell anyone, will you?'

'Cross my heart,' says Lottie.

Topsy pops her head through the kitchen hatch. 'Tell anyone what?'

Apart from Mrs Topping's blue hairnet, they look exactly the same.

'Well, my Trevor, that's Emmeline's pop – he was a spy until they got him.'

Lottie's eyes widen. '*Got him?*'

Cook sniffs over a bowl of washing-up. 'Close your ears, Emmie. They found him in the hippo enclosure in London Zoo.' She shakes her head. 'They're only pygmies, but he was a small man. I was heartbroken, as you can imagine. A hungry little girl to feed and no qualifications except a Brownie badge in crime prevention. That's when O, bless his heart, gave us a roof over our heads and took me on as cook. Turns out I had a talent I never knew about. Mince pie?'

'Um, no thanks . . .'

Filipp whines in my ear. 'Why are you wasting time here? The Scarlet Slippers are just one week away. You should be rehearsing.'

'But I've been dancing all morning.'

'Your Lilac Fairy needs more practice. You still have an hour until kung fu with the Captain. *I* will teach you if I must.'

'S'all right,' says Lottie. 'I know an expert. Hey, Nora. We need your help!'

Nora Doone moves like a flower in the breeze.

'The Lilac Fairy is a *storyteller*,' she says. 'Her moves are expressive. *Languid*. Like this . . .'

Filipp sulks in the corner of the studio. 'I don't see

why you need *her* to teach you when you've got *me*.'

'Lottie – do you wish to turn me off?' says Nora.

'No!' I say.

'Don't take no notice of Filipp, Nora. You carry on.'

'Very well. It's your turn now, Milly. Remember to take your time.'

Filipp walks through Nora and poses in front of me. 'Like *this*.' He steps forward on his left foot and *piqués* on his right in a wonky *arabesque*.

'One movement should really *flow* to the next,' says Nora.

I try to copy her but Filipp struts between us. 'Think *river*. Think *Danube*. Not Niagara Falls! No, no, no. Your expression is like this.' He scrunches his face like an old tissue. 'My m-mother always says you must never show people how you feel. We dancers must hide the effort, the pain, the fear. This is a *performance*. We are *performers*. We perform. Or die.'

I force a smile at Lottie and try not to die.

With five minutes to change for the Captain's class, I leave Lottie and hurry past the biggest Christmas tree I've ever seen. Topsy is on a stepladder, untangling fairy lights and howling 'Do They Know It's Christmas?' at the top of her lungs.

Outside in the courtyard, specks of sleet stick to my hair. Danny and Fleur jog past without saying hello.

'*Pssst . . .*'

A hand tugs me into the archway.

'Merv, what are you doing?'

'Shhh. Can't talk here.'

'I haven't seen you for ages.'

'Been sleeping in the control room,' he says, rubbing his eyes.

'It shows,' says Filipp.

Merv shoves his hand in his pocket and the next thing I know, Filipp has gone. 'This way. Hurry!'

'Did you do that?'

'Do what?'

'Make Filipp go away?'

'Stop asking questions. Come on!' Merv sprints in a very un-Merv-like way towards the trees. 'Merv, we've got kung fu with the Captain. We're going to be late.'

'The Captain can wait.'

Merv throws himself against a tree trunk and rests his hands on his knees.

'Are you going to tell me what's going on?'

He puffs and wipes his forehead. 'I'm being followed.'

I glance around. It's just me, Merv and the trees. 'Followed? Who's following you?'

'I don't know, but there are two of them. I think they might be sixth years.'

'Why would a couple of sixth years be following you?'

'Because Ms Celia told them to. She thinks I'm a mole.'

'Are you joking?'

'I never joke. The control room's been searched too. I don't wear aftershave but this morning it ponged of eau de sixth year. Kydd, why are you looking at me like that?'

'Merv, you haven't done anything silly, have you?'

'What do you mean?'

'*Are* you a mole?'

Merv swipes his little pink nose with his fingerless mittens, shakes his black hair and blinks. 'Do I look like a mole?' I stare at my feet. 'OF COURSE I'M NOT A MOLE! There ISN'T a mole.'

'So why are you telling me all this?'

'I want you to look after something for me.' Merv does a swivelly thing with his eyes and looks over his shoulder. He presses a small brown envelope in my hand. 'Hide it, please.'

'What's this?'

'My life's work. I don't want them to find it.'

'What is it?'

'I can't tell you.'

'Merv, you can't expect me to hide something without telling me what it is.'

Merv sighs. 'You wouldn't understand.'

'Probably not, but I'll try.'

Merv inspects the trees for hidden microphones. 'It's a very sophisticated jammer.'

'Uh?'

'Basically, it stops electrical stuff working. It can make you invisible to electronic surveillance too. It's like a digital invisibility cloak.'

'Wow.'

'I know. It's called *Merv's Universal Magnetic Blocker*. MUMB for short. I've been testing MUMB since we got here. It's still slightly unpredictable.'

'Has MUMB got anything to do with the security cameras not working?'

Merv nods miserably. 'That's why Ms Celia thinks I'm a mole.'

'You mean that stuff you said about teething troubles was a lie? Why don't you just tell her?'

'Don't you see? If Ms Celia gets her hands on MUMB, she'll pass it to Madge Little to develop. I'll get sidelined faster than you can say "Merv Crump is a twelve-year-old nobody from Nowheresville". It's taken me five years to get this far. Once I'm done,

Madge can have it, but until then, it's mine to perfect.' Merv padlocks his satchel and turns back towards the school.

'Merv!' I scramble after him. 'It's Christmas soon. Why don't you just take MUMB home with you?'

Merv hrumphs. 'I'm not going home.'

'But what about your mum?'

'She doesn't care about me. The day I came here she moved to Bovey Tracey with an Elvis impersonator called Ray.'

'Oh, Merv. I'm sure she cares about you. Of course she does.'

'Do you know what she gave me for my last birthday? Superman underpants, I don't think she was being ironic. Anyway, I don't mind staying here. It's a lot cleaner than Ray's flat *and* there's a live-in nurse. Did you know that more people die at Christmas than at any other time of year?'

'No, Merv. I didn't. Look, I'll hide MUMB in my music box for a couple of days, but that's all.'

'NOT IN YOUR MUSIC BOX. It's the most obvious place.'

'Fine, can we just go back? I'm freezing.'

As we cross the hall, Merv leaps behind the Christmas tree.

'What is it?'

'They're there. They just went in the loos.'

'Who? Where?'

'Them,' Merv whispers. 'The sixth-year boys I told you about. They just walked past.'

'You mean those two little old ladies?'

'It was them. Same height. Same shaped heads.' He shuffles down the corridor.

'Merv, they were cleaners. They went in the girls' loos.'

'Believe me. It was the same boys. Every time I see them they're in a different disguise but they can't fool me.' Merv shuffles away. 'Remember, Kydd, MUMB's the word . . .'

'Merv . . . Merv! What about kung fu? Merv!'

I'm going to be late but I have no choice but to rush back to the dorm and hide Merv's MUMB the best I can.

21

The Stars of Tomorrow

'Wakey, wakey, Milly. Guess who's coming to dinner?'

I bolt up and Morris slides off my face.

'KOROLEV!' Today I get to see the man who stole Mum. Tomorrow I get to save her. I leap out of bed and yank on my clothes.

Willow rolls her eyeballs. 'Personally, I don't know what all the excitement's about. If Spencer's mentor is anything to go by, Ivan Korolev wouldn't say boo to a swan. I couldn't care less about the mission anyway. O shouldn't have gotten himself kidnapped in the first place. He can't be a very good spy, can he?'

I wonder if Willow'd say that if she knew O was Mum? She witters on as she brushes her hair. 'It's the Scarlet Slippers that really matter. Madame said if something happens to you, we might have a chance of winning. Did you hear me, Milly? If *I* was dancing, the trophy would be ours.'

What can I say? I totally agree.

I escape Willow and go to find Lottie.

The courtyard is frostier than Madame. I slip on the icy cobbles and Filipp laughs. Careful not to knock the little holly wreath, I tap on Lottie's door.

'Come in!' shouts Lottie. 'Fleur and Dipti have gone for breakfast, but I'm too excited to eat!'

I watch her bounce around the dorm. It looks like she's already put her foot though a lampshade. Nora is on the rug, stretching like a see-through cat. Filipp sits next to her and starts stretching too. He's so competitive.

'Korolev's goin' to wish he never set eyes on your mum!' says Lottie.

At the mention of Mum, my worries gush out. 'Oh, Lottie, what if Kristina won't tell me where Mum is? What if she doesn't trust me?'

'Who could blame her?' says Filipp to Nora.

Lottie jumps on the bed. 'Course she will. She'd never have gone to all this trouble to bottle it at the last minute. When are you meetin' her?'

'I don't know yet. And I've got to get through my Lilac Fairy first. What if I mess up? What if Kristina pulls out? What if Korolev catches us? There are so many things that could go wrong!'

Lottie karate chops the wall. 'Oops.' She pats a dent in the plasterwork.

I grab her ankle. 'Let's go, before you break anything else.'

Once I've got Lottie outside, she points past the courtyard to the frosty, white lawn. 'Will you look at that? First they turn the assault course into a football pitch and now there's a tennis court where the shootin' range used to be. I hate flamin' tennis.'

'They're just trying to make Swan House look like an ordinary school, Lottie. They don't want the Van Twinkles to guess what goes on here.'

'I know. But *tennis*!' Her sigh hovers in the freezing air.

Fillip runs after us as we cut through the refectory. Extra tables have been brought in for the Scarlet Supper tonight. The year sevens are busy covering them in red velvet tablecloths.

I dodge a trolley. 'So much has happened, I can't believe I've only been here for one term.'

'But we ain't *done* nuffink yet,' says Lottie. 'If I have to practise one more *chaîné*, I'll . . . Flamin' Nora, what the Scarlet Supper's *that*?'

We stand aside as Cook wheels a giant cake out of the kitchen. It's covered in lumpy grey icing and the decoration on top looks like a brown marzipan boat.

'That looks nice,' I say, practising my unreadable spy face.

Cook beams. 'I hope they like it. Took me ages to make that Scarlet Slipper.'

Lottie pinches my arm. 'What's in it?' I ask.

'Ooo, it's my secret recipe, so you won't tell anyone, will you?'

'Scout's honour,' says Lottie.

'You weren't in Scouts,' I whisper.

'I know,' says Lottie.

'Well, there's flour, of course. And eggs. And chocolate. And let me see . . . cornflakes for crunch. Turnips. Mayonnaise. And anchovies. Just enough to give that *je ne sais quoi*. Topsy says it's the best cake I've ever made.'

Lottie honks through her nose.

I take her away.

In the corridor, we dodge two fifth years taking off their ice skates. Spencer goes by with a pair of Nordic skis. Ivan Korolev trails behind him reciting from the *Guide to Espionage*. It's hard to walk in a straight line without bumping into someone doing something important.

'Uh-oh,' I say. 'We'd better help Topsy.'

Over at the reception, Topsy is balancing on the top rung of a stepladder.

'Neeeearly . . . there . . .' She stretches across the

desk. The ladder starts to wobble.

Luckily, the Captain arrives just in time to catch her. 'I'll take that, pet.' He doesn't even have to stand on tiptoes to pin the banner in place.

Topsy turns fuchsia. 'Thank you, Captain. What do you think of my banner? I made it myself.'

The Captain stands back and his straw-coloured eyebrows knit together. '*Welcome to Swan House*,' he reads. '*Hosts of the Scarlet Slipper Ballet Prize. Honk-honk!*' The banner is decorated with baby swans and little pink love hearts.

'It's – it's – help us, girls.'

'As lovely as your mum's cake?' says Lottie.

'Well said, Li.' The Captain turns to Topsy. 'If that's all you need, pet, I've got to check the theatre.'

Topsy sighs as the Captain strides away. 'He's like Mummy's chocolate pudding. Hard on the outside and all melty in the middle.'

Lottie coughs.

'Sorry. What was that, Lottie?'

'Uhh, we got time before our last rehearsal. Can we do anyfink to help?'

'Let me see – no. I've just got to make the place cards and I'll be nearly-almost done.'

Lottie and I head for class, but as we round the corner, she yanks me back. I signal to Filipp to stay beside me. Outside the studio, Madame is whispering with Ms Celia.

'Do not weaken now, Celia,' says Madame. 'Ze evidence is clear.'

'I wish I shared your certainty, Blanche. The closer we get to the competition, the more concerned I am that Garth may be right and we've made a dreadful mistake.' Madame takes Ms Celia's arm and the doors bang shut behind them.

'Are they still going on about a mole?' says Lottie.

'Sounds like it,' I say.

Which reminds me, I should check on Merv later. I haven't seen him for a week.

Five minutes later, everyone else arrives and we trail them into the studio.

Madame claps her hands. 'Fleur, stop talking. To ze barre, *tout le monde*.'

Ms Celia waits while we warm up, then everybody watches as I run through my Lilac Fairy. But I'm not thinking about my dance. I'm thinking about her conversation with Madame. I don't understand. The Scarlet Supper is tonight. She should be talking about Korolev. She should be talking about the mission. She should be talking about Mum.

When I've finished, Madame waves me back to the barre. 'You are dancing like a robot,' she says. 'It will be a miracle if we are taken seriously as a school of ballet. Don't you agree, Ms Celia?'

'O once told me that miracles can only be achieved with patience and kindness, Madame.'

Mum's words are wasted on Madame. '*Patience and kindness* are luxuries we cannot afford.'

'Then we must agree to disagree,' says Ms Celia. 'All right, everyone. Please take your positions for *Romeo and Juliet*.'

We all get into our lines. Miss Batty thumps out 'The Dance of the Knights' on the piano and my spine tingles with every foreboding note. Fleur yelps when I bump into her and Willow rolls her eyes.

Ms Celia sighs. 'Milly, please try and concentrate. The rest of you, well done.'

Madame's eyes say 'I told you so'. She calls me and Danny to the centre. 'And now for ze final *pas de deux*. Remember your core, Millicent. We do not want any *accidents* zis close to ze competition.'

I glance at Danny. There are four lifts in our *pas de deux*. Four 'accidents' waiting to happen.

The music begins. Every time Danny takes my waist, I tense my core and wait to be dropped. At the end, he whispers in my ear, 'I promised you could trust me, and I meant it. But only when we're *onstage*.'

'That was better, Milly,' says Ms Celia. Thank you, boys and girls, I think you are ready. *Cycni venustas, cor leonis!*'

Everyone cheers except me. 'The schools will be here shortly, and as the refectory is being prepared for this evening, Cook has made a picnic lunch, which you can eat in Studio Four. Off you go. You too, Milly – I'll see you later.'

Lottie takes my arm. 'Don't listen to Madame. You got to believe in yourself. You deserve to dance in the Scarlet Slippers, don't she, Spence?'

'Absolutely,' says Spencer, who's playing with his Swanphone and not listening.

'Who will be judging with my grandm-mother?' asks Filipp.

'Your mum, I fink,' answers Lottie.

'My m-mother?' Filipp blinks. 'Will she see me?'

'No chance,' says Lottie. 'We got to turn off our mentors while there's visitors here.'

Filipp tries to prod me with a see-though finger. 'You do know my m-mother is impossible to please. If you'd listened to me you wouldn't be such an embarrassment.'

I open my mouth to reply but Spencer butts in. 'Kydd, do you want the good news, or the good news?'

'The good news?'

'You can turn Popov off now. Because *a coach has just been spotted pulling into the park!*'

Filipp opens his mouth to argue, but for once I

don't have to listen. At that moment, one of the year seven girls crashes into the studio. 'THEY'RE HERE! THE VAN TWINKLES. THEY'RE HERE!'

Spencer shakes his head. 'Year sevens – they're so excitable.' But seconds later, he's hurtling into the hall with everyone else.

Madame is standing guard at the entrance. '*Arrêtez!* Do you forget zis is a school of *ballet*? Unless you are part of ze welcoming party, stand back from ze door. Dipti Patel – is zat your mentor? Turn her off IMMEDIATELY!'

Lottie hooks her arm primly though mine. ''Ead up, Millicent,' she says in the worst French accent I've ever heard. 'Shouldeurs back! 'Ave you forgotten we are *ballerinas*?' She grabs my arm. 'Quick! Best view's from the studio next door.'

The studio is quiet but I hold Lottie back. In the window is a Viking silhouette. Captain holds a puckered fingertip to his lips and heaves up the sash.

The noise of an engine rumbles through the trees. A flash of silver glints through the branches and the largest coach I've ever seen rolls up the driveway. Painted on the side under a swooshing shooting star is *Van Twinkle's Stars of Tomorrow*. Dozens of small noses squish against the windows.

Ms Celia and Madame wait in the porch as the bus pulls up in front of the steps. First to get off is a man in a white suit and a large, white cowboy hat. He's as round as one of the Captain's exercise balls.

He holds out his arms and darts up the steps. 'Blanche! May I say, you're as a bewitching now as you were the day we met.' He kisses Madame's hand like she's the queen. 'Uh, you too, Celia, honey.'

'I wish I could say the same about you, Dick,' says Ms Celia.

'Nice place you have here, girls.' He hooks his thumbs in the belt hidden under his tummy. 'No sign of Ivan?'

'Mr Korolev will be joining us later.'

'We'll show him, eh, ladies? Still can't figure how he managed to worm his way back into the competition.'

Dick Van Twinkle gestures at the children stepping off the bus. 'So, here are my babies. Ain't they something?' His voice cracks. 'They make me so proud.'

Two by two, the children approach the steps and curtsy to Madame.

Lottie shakes her head. 'You'd fink they'd arrived at Buckin'am flamin' Palace.'

'This is so priddy!' says one. 'What a cute little pond. And are those real?' She points at the swans.

Ms Celia tuts.

The last two children are like a pair of beautiful black swans. They have the same black skin, long necks and determined faces.

'Ladies, my brightest students,' says Dick Van Twinkle. 'Only one word to describe 'em. The Stars of Tomorrow.'

'That's four words, Dick,' says Ms Celia.

I whisper to Lottie, 'How can I compete with the Stars of Tomorrow?'

Dick Van Twinkle puts his arms around them. 'Sorry, ladies. These two are gonna dance right out of here with the trophy.' Then he pulls a silk handkerchief from his pocket and dabs his eyes. 'Only one word to describe their talent. Outta This World.'

Ms Celia sighs.

'Please, monsieur,' says Madame. 'Come inside.'

Topsy appears behind Madame. 'HELLOOO, Mr Van Twinkle. This way, please-thank-you. AND YOU, TWINKLETS!'

'Geez Louise!' says Dick Van Twinkle. 'Who is *this*?'

'This is Emmeline,' says Ms Celia. 'She'll look after you while you're here. You've had a long journey. I'm sure a wash and brush up are in order. When you're ready, I'll show you the practice studios.'

Topsy pops something around Dick Van Twinkle's neck.

'What was that, Captain?' asks Lottie.

'A special visitor's pass,' says the Captain. 'It's tagged, so we know what our guests are getting up to. In extreme circumstances it also self-destructs, but I don't think we need to worry about that right now.'

'Mummy said to tell you she's your biggest fan!' says Topsy to Dick Van Twinkle.

She turns fuchsia again when he kisses her hand. 'In that case, lead the way, Emmie. I'll say this for you Brits – you sure know talent when you see it.'

'Dick,' adds Ms Celia. 'Please be aware, this is an old building. For your own safety, avoid the areas that are off limits to visitors.'

'Hey, we like "old", don't we kids? "Old" is what you Brits do best.'

'Dick. That wasn't a request.'

Dick Van Twinkle tips his hat. 'Like I said, Celia. You ain't changed a bit.'

22

The Scarlet Supper

Topsy leads the Americans away and I watch the welcoming party scatter. Lottie is still peering out over the lawn. 'When is Korolev goin' to get here, Captain?'

The Captain closes the window. 'Crump is monitoring the coach. It should be here in time for the Scarlet Supper tonight.'

'So, what do we do until then?'

'Keep your eyes open. If any of the Americans get lost, direct them back to their rooms. But go easy. They have no idea what's going on here and we don't want anyone ending up in the infirmary, got it?'

'Got it.'

'Good lass, off you go. Kydd, you're coming with us.'

Madge Little peeks out of the shoe cupboard as we go past. Her small pink fingers flutter over her lips. 'Oh dear, is there a problem with the visitor passes?'

'What was that, Madge?'

'The passes, Captain.'

'Don't worry, Madge. They haven't self-destructed yet.'

'In that case, I'm going for a nap before supper. That flying tutu's giving me sleepless nights.'

'Did she just say *flying* tutu?' I ask, but the Captain doesn't seem to be listening.

'Sorry, what was that, pet?'

If I didn't know better, I'd say he was away with the bliddy fairies.

The Captain comes to an abrupt stop outside the gym. 'In you go – Ms Celia's asked me to give you a final brief.'

The door clicks behind us. All of the targets and dummies are gone. The Captain perches on the edge of a balance beam. He shifts his weight and the beam groans.

'You've studied Kristina Kovalchuk's file?'

'Yes. I've been swotting up on her for ages.'

'Good. Tonight at supper, watch her closely. If she doesn't give you a signal to abort, you'll meet with her after your performance tomorrow.'

'Where should I go?'

'I'm coming to that. As soon as you've finished

dancing, go straight to Madame's study. At midnight, Kristina will join you. She'll then reveal your mother's location. She's insisted that you remove your Swanphone before the meeting, so remember to give it to Madame before the performance. Any questions?'

'You mentioned a signal?'

'A signal? Oh aye. If Kristina has to pull out, she'll blow her nose. Right, I've got a posh dinner to get ready for. Tying a bow tie with these fingers might take us all night.' He takes my shoulders. 'Do exactly as I've said and you'll be all right. Do you understand, pet? *Exactly* as I've said.'

As I leave the gym, the Captain's sigh rumbles in my ears.

Lottie is waiting for me outside the dorm. She's already changed into the uniform Madge has made especially for the Scarlet Supper; a soft white dress and pale-blue wrap cardigan.

'Quick, Milly, open the door before I turn into an ice lolly. Don't know why we have to wear flamin' uniform tonight.'

'At least it's not as itchy as the horrible brown jumpers in St Tild—'

My words are lost in a loud whirr. Lottie's hair flies up and her skirt flaps against her legs. Light floods the courtyard in a swirl of snowflakes. The noise gets louder and I clamp my hands over my ears.

I look up to see a big, black shape sweep towards the roof of the octagon.

'What's that?'

Lottie shouts a reply, but I can't hear a word. She pushes me inside the dorm and shuts out the noise. 'I said it's the judges! Dame Anna and Olga Popova. They're here! Milly – it's happenin'. Tomorrow you're goin' to find your mum!'

By the time I've changed, the Popovs' helicopter has landed. As we cross the courtyard, snowflakes settle on Lottie's black hair. She slows under the arch and takes my arm. I'm trembling, but not because of the cold. 'What if Kristina doesn't show up? The Casovans aren't even here yet.'

'Yes they are,' grunts a figure in the shadows. 'I've just overseen a two-hour bus search.'

'Merv! I've been worried about you.' Merv's monobrow is iced with snow.

'Why've you been worried about *Merv*?' says Lottie.

'I'll explain later. You searched their bus?'

'It activated the alarms when it went past the gate house, but it was only the driver. He had nine metal fillings.'

'I hate the flamin' dentist,' says Lottie with a shudder.

Merv jerks to a stop like a supermarket trolley with a dodgy wheel.

'What's wrong?' I ask.

'I told you the first day of term; I don't do refectories.'

'But Merv, you can't miss the Scarlet Supper. Come on, you can sit with us.'

Merv stomps around for a bit and has a little argument with himself. '*No, yes, no, yes, nooo-kaaay.*'

'Does he *have* to?' says Lottie.

I squeeze Lottie's arm as we enter the refectory. It's exactly how I imagined the Capulets' grand ballroom. The tables are laid with red velvet tablecloths and decorated with holly and ivy. The crystal chandeliers make everything look sparkly and exciting. Even Merv.

All the teachers are gathered at a long top table. At the centre sits Ms Celia. On her left are the Captain and Madge Little. On her right are Madame, Dame Anna and a woman with a long neck and longer nose. She looks down it at the Scarlet Slipper sculpture. Olga Popova. It's weird to think she's Filipp's mum. At either end of the table is an empty chair.

Lottie nudges my arm. In the middle of the table glistens a Scarlet Slipper, carved in ice.

We find our table. Next to each napkin is a name card written in Topsy's handwriting. Lottie flashes one of them under my nose. *Kristina Kovalchuk*.

Merv finds Spencer's card and drops it on the table behind us. He plonks himself in Spencer's seat, picks up a bread roll and inspects it for germs. I sink into my chair and wonder if Kristina will be watching me as closely as I'll be watching her.

Lottie picks up a roll too. 'Reminds me of my cousin's weddin',' she says, showing Merv the gap in her teeth.

Merv's eyebrow twitches. 'You had a fight? At a *wedding*?'

'What do you take me for?' says Lottie. 'The cake was worse than Cook's and I lost my tooth in the icin'. Got to get it sorted in the Christmas holidays but I hate the flamin' dentist.' She bangs the roll on the table and all the glasses clink. 'I wish everyone would get a move on. I want to get a look at Korolev.'

'Korolev's not here,' says Merv. 'Wasn't on the bus. No one knows where he is.'

Before Merv can explain, a fanfare sounds.

'Shame – it's only Van Twinkletoes,' says Lottie.

Dick Van Twinkle twirls between the tables. He's wearing a silver three-piece suit with matching silver cowboy boots. Twirling behind him, in red, white and blue, are the Stars of Tomorrow. It's like a Fourth of July parade.

Dick joins the teachers at the top table. The Stars of Tomorrow mill between us looking for their names.

'Hi, y'all,' says a girl with the most perfect teeth I've ever seen. 'I'm Bonnie Rae Bridges and this is my friend, Kimmy. Looks like we'll be joining your table tonight. It's a pleasure to meet y'all.'

Kimmy has the second most perfect teeth I've ever seen.

'Bread roll, Bonnie?' says Lottie.

Bonnie's teeth are saved by a noise outside. The doors crash open and everyone cranes their necks.

'It's Korolev's lot!' says Lottie. 'I'm goin' to get a closer look.' She dives under the table.

Korolev's students swoop through the doors like moths. The boys wear swooshy black capes. The girls wear swooshy red skirts. Their waistcoats are embroidered in gold.

I recognize some of them from Kristina's file. The boy with the scar (hobbies: pickpocketing and parkour). The girl with the fox-red hair (poker and ping-pong). Behind them all is a girl with ruby lips and roving eyes.

Kristina the Knife, my new best friend.

Kristina and the boy with the scar head our way. Kristina's thick yellow plaits are piled on top of her head. She reads each of the name cards and takes the seat opposite me.

'You are Milly?' she says in perfect English. I breathe out. She definitely doesn't look like a 'crim'. 'Who's your friend?'

'Oh, this is Merv.'

Merv produces a straw from his satchel and takes a slurp of water.

Kristina wrinkles her nose and turns to the bay. Got to keep the conversation going . . . 'I love your hair, Kristina.'

'Thank you. I like yours also.'

'Do you? Thanks.' This is a good start. Lottie says my hair has grown a bit, but not necessarily in the right direction.

Kristina stops smiling. 'I was being sarcastic, *hlúpe*.'

Did Kristina just call me stupid? I try to think of an extremely intelligent reply, but it comes out as 'duh'.

Bonnie Rae Bridges puts down her butter knife. 'It sure is nice to meet you, Miss . . . ?

'Kristina,' snarls Kristina.

'You know, Krissie, honey – if we make friends at this here competition, it won't matter who takes home the little ol' Scarlet Slipper cos we'll all be winners.'

Bonnie smiles and I nudge her bread roll off the table. It would be a shame if she lost one of her perfect teeth.

Kristina reaches for her knife and Merv whimpers, 'Bad start. Very. Bad. Start.'

She starts talking to the boy in Casovan. 'We are going to win the Scarlet Slipper without even trying.'

The boy rubs his scar. 'I hope you're right, Kristina. It's time Ivan got his precious trophy. Perhaps then he'll stop being so hard on us.'

'We've got Vilppu to blame for that.'

'Vilppu was a joke.' The boy scowls as Lottie's head pops up from under the table. She crawls up her chair leg and brushes herself down.

We communicate by eyebrow. *Have you seen Korolev?* ask mine.

He's not here, say hers.

Are you sure? say mine.

Definitely, say hers.

But Lottie is wrong.

The door flies open.

The room draws breath.

Kristina drops her knife.

It quivers in the table.

But not as much as me. Standing in the doorway is the man who turned my world upside down. Back to front. Inside out. He sweeps his cape around his shoulders and shakes his bluebottle-black head.

Ivan, our friend, has gone. Korolev, our enemy, sighs.

'How disappointing,' he says in a voice soaked in poison. 'I see you've started thc party vithout me.'

23

The Wicked Fairy

The name *Korolev* bounces off the polished glass and twinkling chandeliers. It passes from table to table in an excited whisper. It smacks Merv in the face.

Kristina Kovalchuk laughs without smiling. 'If you thought he vasn't coming, you don't know Ivan Korolev. He vouldn't miss this for the vorld!'

'Reminds me of Carabosse, the bad fairy in *Sleepin' Beauty*,' whispers Lottie.

'How did he get in?' says Merv in a very small voice. 'How did he get in?'

I nod at the top table. 'Looks like the Captain's asking himself the same question.'

The Captain is gripping the tablecloth like he's about to perform a magic trick. I think I hear his teeth gnashing together. Madame's smile is frozen to her face. Next to her, Dame Anna's lips are pressed together in a line of even blanket stitch.

Ms Celia rises from her chair. Her forehead gives nothing away. 'You are late, Mr Korolev.'

'*Ivan*, please, Celia.' Korolev takes his seat next to Dame Anna. 'Don't look so afraid, old woman. I promise not to bite.'

I don't notice the year sevens bringing out the first course until the soup bowls are plonked on the table.

They don't splosh.

'Cook says she hopes you enjoy tonight's menu,' announces our waitress, without taking her eyes off Korolev. 'She says to tell you she's made *a selection of British classics for your de-lec-tation*.'

'Oh my,' says Bonnie. 'I've heard so much about your British food . . . fish 'n' chips . . . Yorkshire pudding . . . chicken tikka masala . . .'

Kristina and Lottie are eyeball wrestling across the table. Lottie blinks first and starts eating her soup with a knife and fork. 'Old British custom,' she says to a bewildered Kimmy.

'What's in it? No, don't tell me,' says Merv.

'Jellied eel, ain't it,' says Lottie happily. 'Never had it in a soup before but it ain't bad once you get used to it.'

I can't stop staring at Korolev. His presence fills the room like fire. Get too close and poor Dame Anna will get burnt.

The main course arrives. According to our year seven waitress, it's steak and kidney pie.

'These are . . . *interestin'*,' says Bonnie. She holds up a wrinkly black blob on her fork. 'What are they?'

'Offal,' says Merv.

'They ain't *that* bad,' says Lottie.

On the top table, Korolev eats like a wolf. He pours Filipp's mother some wine. She waits for Korolev to take a sip before picking up her glass.

While Lottie's eating, I listen to Kristina and the boy talking in Casovan. If I didn't know Kristina was on our side, it would be difficult to tell which one of them is the most demented.

'If I was a student here, I would drown the cook in the lake like a kitten,' says the boy.

Kristina replies, 'I would throw a knife through her stupid blue hairnet.'

'Ha!' says the boy. 'Right between the eyes. This is why you and I get along so well, Kristina. We understand each other.'

Just as well Lottie doesn't speak Casovan.

Our waitress bangs down the pudding. 'Cook's special, "Swan" Mess.'

'Can I go now?' says Merv.

Merv and I haven't touched our food, and neither has Kristina. She picks up her napkin. It hovers near her nose and I try not to stare. Please, *please* don't blow.

She snarls at me and drops her napkin on the floor. You've got to give it to her; Kristina really is an excellent actress. No one would ever suspect she wanted to help us. I give her a little thumbs up when no one's looking.

Cook wheels out the cake. The *ooos* are followed by *urghs*. Lottie snorts meringue on Kimmy. Cook goes for a lie-down.

Kristina absent-mindedly plays with her knife.

When everyone has finished not eating, Dick Van Twinkle rises to his feet and chimes the side of his glass. 'I'd like to say a few words, if my friend, Ms Celia, will let me?'

'If you must, Dick.'

'Thank you, Celia. Ladies and gentlemen, friends and colleagues, boys and girls, you have no idea what a thrill this is. To be here, in London, England with you guys –' he waves at Madame – 'and you guys –' he waves at Korolev – 'to see *the ballet* bring people together.' He dabs an eye with his napkin. 'The power of dance, people. It's a wonderful thing.'

Korolev rises to his feet and starts to clap. Slowly, people join in.

'Vell said, my friend. And so, ladies and gentlemen, vould you please join me in toasting our hosts.

To Svan House School of Ballet and the Scarlet Slippers.'

'To Swan House School of Ballet,' says Ms Celia. '*Cycni venustas, cor leonis.*'

Korolev raises his glass. '*Pijem liške, ktorá obidvoch obviní!*'

To the grace of a swan, the heart of a lion. And the fox who will outwit them both.

24

The Return of the Lilac Fairy

After the Scarlet Supper, I lie awake all night. Tomorrow I have to dance the Lilac Fairy perfectly. If I don't, Kristina will think I'm a joke, like that boy she mentioned, Vilppu. And if she thinks I'm a joke, she might not come to our rendezvous. At least I have Mum's homing shoes. They won't let me down.

At six o'clock, my wrist glows. I've got two messages. One from Topsy saying that, because Meekes are short-staffed, our shoes won't be delivered until this afternoon. And one from Merv with two words. *Come outside*.

I rub my eyes and tell myself not to worry – he probably just wants his MUMB back.

Willow's head is buried under her duvet. I tug on as many clothes as possible before opening the door. The cold air snaps at my nose and fingertips.

Merv is wearing a snowsuit. 'Follow me.'

'OK, but this better be quick.'

I pull on my beret and traipse after him. A thin carpet of snow muffles the sound of our feet. Little white drifts are piled around the trees. 'Merv, stop. I'm not going any further until you tell me what this is about.'

'It's about the mole,' he says.

'Merv, I've got enough to worry about, without worrying about you worrying about a mole.'

'This is important, Kydd. I thought Ms Celia only believed there was a mole because of MUMB disrupting the security cameras. But I was wrong. Last night I discovered there actually *is* a mole and Ms Celia's hoping to catch him tonight.'

'But we're supposed to be looking for my mum tonight.'

'That's why I'm here. The mole must be a serious threat to the success of the mission. You need to be careful. It could be the same person who tried to poison you. They could be dangerous. Very.'

My teeth begin to chatter. 'D-do you think the mole is one of us, Merv? D-do you think it could possibly be . . . *Willow Perkins*?'

'Why would I think that?'

'Well, Mum wrote a *W* on the programme.'

Merv pulls a sheet of paper from his satchel. 'There are two reasons why that is completely illogical. First, on the night your mum was kidnapped, Willow *hadn't been recruited to Swan House*. And second, the *W* isn't a *W*.'

'Oh.'

'Besides, if it was Willow, why wouldn't your mum just have circled her in the picture? I examined the programme and an indentation on the paper indicates that your mum's pen ran out.' He hands me a printout.

Mum's *W* has been blown up. There are scratches underneath that join up with the *W* to make a shape. An unmistakable shape.

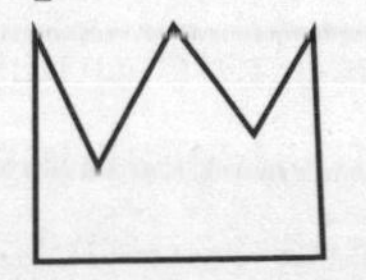

Merv's right. The *W* is not a *W*. It's not even a letter.

It's a crown.

'It could be an important clue. I've been looking at the semiotics and there are several possible meanings of crowns—'

'I know what it means.'

'It could relate to our own royal fam—'

'Merv, I know what it means!'

'You do?'

'It means I've wasted your time. Sorry. All Mum was trying to tell us is the name of her kidnapper and we already know that.'

'But . . .'

'*Korolev*. Translated into English it means *Crown*.'

'Oh,' says Merv. 'Why didn't I think of that?'

'Merv, I'd really like to go back now. It's not easy dancing the Lilac Fairy with frostbite.'

I tiptoe back inside the dorm. All I can do is hope Merv is wrong. If the mole blows the mission, I might never see Mum again.

Back in school, the excitement from last night's Scarlet Supper has turned into quiet concentration. All the competitors are rehearsing in their studios. Lottie's with Ms Celia and the rest of the *corps de ballet*, while I'm stuck with Madame and Willow. Even Dafydd Wynn-Jones seems nervous. I'm taking a break near reception when a delivery arrives from Meekes. I'm glad to see a friendly face.

Pip is stacking boxes on the desk. 'Hello, Miss Millicent. Sorry I can't chat. Busy day. Got to get back to Meekes, pick up the last of the shoes and drive back out again with the Scarlet Slipper trophy.'

I cross my fingers. 'It's OK, Pip. I just wondered if you knew how Mr Stubbs is doing?'

The freckles on Pip's forehead squash together. 'Nothing's changed, miss. He's still in hospital. If I hear anything, I'll let you know.'

'OK,' I say, not sounding at all OK.

'I hope you like your shoes, miss. They're not as good as Heart Maker's but I tried my best.'

'Thanks, Pip, I'm sure they'll be perfect.' I haven't got the heart to tell him I'll be wearing Mum's homing shoes tonight.

As Pip rushes away, a Casovan shout escapes the studio opposite.

'No one is going to stand betveen Ivan Korolev and the Scarlet Slipper this time! Especially not you, Kristina. Again – from the beginning!' Korolev's voice drops to a menacing growl. 'Don't let me down, my dear. I hate it when people let me down.'

Blimey. No wonder Kristina wants to help us. On my way back to our studio, I make sure to touch Dame Anna's statue.

The afternoon whirls by and in no time at all it's time to collect my Lilac Fairy tutu from wardrobe. Waiting on the rail next to it is my Odette costume for the *pas de deux*. Small white feathers cover the skirt and the bodice sparkles with rhinestones. The tiny pearls on the eye mask are like tears.

I think of Mum and make a silent promise not to let her down.

Soon darkness swallows up the lawn and the driveway fills with cars. Ms Celia directs the TV crew into the theatre.

All I need are Mum's homing shoes but when I open the box, it's empty.

There's only one person who would have taken them. I fling down the lid. Willow ruins everything! But then I hear Mr Stubbs in my head. *Keep dancing*, he says. *Don't let no one stop you.*

Backstage, Topsy's waiting to cover up my lack of hair with white lilacs. Despite everything, the moment my tutu crackles and pops over my head, something magical happens and I feel like a real ballerina again.

I lengthen my neck, suck in my stomach, tuck in my bottom, and *pirouette*.

Once. Twice. Three times . . .

Someone claps behind me.

Ms Celia's nails are scrubbed and clean. She's wearing a dab of rouge and even a smudge of lipstick. 'That was lovely, Milly. I have to confess, I was worried that I'd asked too much of you, but now

I see no reason why the mission won't be a success. With luck, you will be reunited with your mother very soon.'

She leads me into the wings. 'Before you go on, a word of advice. Quite naturally, your main concern is for your mother. But if you can, try to leave your worries in the wings and stay in the moment. You can be certain that whatever's happened in the past and whatever may happen in the future will be waiting for you when you finish. I see a lot of Eva in you, Milly. Make her proud. Make yourself proud.'

She squeezes my arm and I'm on my own. I take my position onstage and place my shaking left foot *tendu devant*.

The theatre sighs with the sound of violins and I let the music fill me up like a cream puff. I forget my burning toes, my achy heart. I forget Ivan Korolev and Willow. I forget the past and the future. I dance for Mum and for me. Nothing else matters.

The last note fades. There's silence. Then someone claps and suddenly there's enough applause to make my teeth chatter. But when I see Ms Celia's face, the cream puff feeling melts away. Her expression is tragic. In her eyes are actual tears. I've never seen Ms Celia cry before, and the sight makes my own tears roll off my nose in actual drips.

I walk offstage and a little sob catches in my throat. 'I'm sorry,' I say. 'My arms were all over the place and my *piqués* were wonky.'

'Not at all. You were wonderful,' says Ms Celia. 'Oh, Milly. I'm sorry.'

'Sorry for what?'

Ms Celia clears her throat. 'Never mind. Hurry now. Go straight to Madame's. Don't delay.'

No one sees me as I run into the hall. No one sees me slip into Madame's study. The only thing to follow me down the corridor is the sound of violins.

I shut the door quietly behind me. But when I switch on the light, I make a sound I've never made before – a sort of gasp-groan-roar.

Madame's cabinet – her precious cabinet – hangs open. The Popovs' heirlooms are smashed all over the floor; an ugly carpet of glass and splinters, satin and pictures.

I have to let someone know, but I gave my Swanphone to Madame! WHAT SHOULD I DO?

I stumble back to the door. Turn the knob. Rattle the knob. Push and twist and shake the knob.

It's locked.

I have a terrible thought. Madame will think I did this.

I have a worse one.

Kristina won't be able to get in. She won't be able to tell me where Mum is . . .

The Captain always says you should never let your emotions get the better of you. He says it's important to keep your head at all times. He says it's better to have a cool head than no head. Huh! I beat the door. Kick the door. Curse the door.

Garghhh. If only I had one of Madge's bobby pins. Think, Milly. Think!

What would a real spy do? I remember Rule Eleven of *The Guide to Espionage* – never discount the obvious. Maybe there's an old-fashioned key somewhere?

I empty the desk drawer and start searching through the contents.

I find a pair of white kid gloves, an ivory comb, pale-blue note paper. But not one old-fashioned key.

The grandfather clock strikes the half hour. Thirty minutes until Kristina comes.

I shake the drawer in frustration.

Something rattles inside.

Rule Twelve of *The Guide to Espionage* – when you have discounted the obvious, look again.

Using the letter opener, I prize the bottom of the drawer away. Sure enough, it's a false bottom. But the only thing inside the hidden compartment is a useless black file.

I throw down the file and out slides a picture of a woman in a beautiful black tutu, topped off with a tiara, sequins and glossy black feathers.

Mum.

Shaking, I pick it up. Underneath the picture and the word 'Odile' is a stamp. TOP SECRET. The signature at the bottom reads, 'Celia Sitwell, DCB'.

As I read on, the words begin to blur.

What I'm reading is a horrible lie.

It can't be true. IT ISN'T TRUE . . .

Ms Celia says the mole isn't Merv.

Ms Celia says it's Mum.

I don't know what Ms Celia's plan is, but somehow, I've got to escape and find Mum before she does.

But first, I've got to calm down. Rule Number Nineteen of *The Guide to Espionage* – panic is the enemy of reason. Deep breaths, Milly, deep breaths.

Huff puff. Huff puff. Huff puff . . .

And then it comes to me. The tunnels. Didn't Spencer say there was a tunnel to Madame's study? All I have to do is find the entrance.

Behind me the grandfather clock chimes again. Quarter to midnight.

Don't discount the obvious.

I push myself up and run my fingers along the case of the clock. I press lightly. There's a click, and the door swings back.

Straight into a startled face.

25

Is it a Merv? Is it a Plane?

'Owww!' says Spencer. 'Careful, Kydd. This nose is a family heirloom.'

'Spencer! What are you doing here? You should be in the theatre. How did you know I was—'

'No time to chat. I'll explain later. You've got to get out of here. Your mum's life might depend on it.'

He shines an old-fashioned torch further inside the grandfather clock. The light rests on a narrow spiral staircase.

I begin to wobble. 'Where does it go?'

'Down to the basement. But it doesn't stop there. Follow me.'

He steps onto a rung of the staircase and grasps both sides. 'Noise travels,' he whispers. 'So, no talking until we get to the bottom.'

Hands sliding, feet slipping, I feel my way down.

Our footsteps echo on the iron treads. Shadows loom and shrink on the walls.

Eventually, Spencer jumps down and helps me to the ground. The top of his head brushes the roof. He stoops as he swings his light in an arc. There are no windows or doors. Just a warren of tunnels disappearing into the gloom.

'Cool, isn't it?' he says. 'Not many people know about these. I'm guessing that's how Korolev got in yesterday.'

There's a grunt in the darkness. 'For the record, I think this is a REALLY BAD IDEA and henceforth, WE ARE ALL DOOMED.'

'*Doomed . . . doomed . . . doomed . . .*' echoes the tunnel.

'*Merv?*'

Someone takes my arm. 'What Merv's tryin' to say is, it ain't good news.'

'*Lottie!*' My skin prickles. 'Have they found Mum already?'

'No. But Ms Celia lied to you.'

'*Lied . . . lied . . . lied . . .*' echoes the tunnel.

'I know, she thinks Mum's the mole.'

'That ain't all,' says Lottie. 'Merv – tell her what you told us.'

Merv ducks. 'Was that a bat? Are there bats down here? I don't know why you dragged me along. I've got a cough and a headache and now I can't breathe properly. Two minutes ago, I forgot the value of pi. I never forget things. NOOOO. It's histoplasmosis! I've got to get out of here.' He sneezes. 'See.'

Spencer grabs Merv by the collar. 'Bad news, Merv. It's more likely to be that other deadly illness . . .'

'What?'

'The COMMON COLD? Now, tell Milly about the stuff on Ms Celia's hard drive!'

Merv sniffs. 'I hacked into Ms Celia's computer and found several files named *Odile*. They were all about Eva. You know your mum was on tour just before she disappeared?'

'Yes – she was away for three weeks.'

'She'd been undercover. Her mission was to identify the mole at Swan House. She was supposed to meet Ms Celia after the Scarlet Slippers, but when she didn't show up, Ms Celia assumed she'd been the mole all along.'

'Everything about Korolev and the kidnap was a lie,' says Spencer.

'Yeah,' says Lottie. 'Kristina was never goin' to tell you where your mum was cos she doesn't have a bleedin' clue. They was all lyin' to you, Ms Celia, Madame, even the Captain.'

So that's why Ms Celia just said she was sorry . . .

'I don't understand. If they thought Mum was a mole, why did they recruit me?'

'Your mum never missed seein' you dance, did she?' says Lottie. 'They used you as *bait*.'

Spencer nods. 'Ms Celia thought if you danced in the Scarlet Slippers, your mum would sneak in to watch. Why do think you were given all the main roles? Problem is, Ms Celia's little plan didn't work. She's not here.'

'So, where *is* she?'

Merv's monobrow shrugs. 'We don't know. I suppose there's still a chance she might turn up. If she *is* the mole.'

'Of course she's not the bleedin' mole,' says Lottie.

Merv backs into the tunnel. 'Why are you all looking so dangerous? I'm only stating the facts.'

'There's somefink else,' says Lottie. 'Ms Celia's got a Plan B. She's pinning all her hopes on Willow Perkins.'

'What?' I say. 'Why Willow?'

'Sorry, Milly. Perkins told Madame that it was *her* your Mum really wanted to see. So now they're goin' to use her as bait. She'll be dancin' your mum's favourite – *Swan Lake* – tomorrow night.'

I slump down on the cold, damp stone and do my very best to fight back the tears. 'I'm going home.'

'We all think you should go to Mr Fly Fishing's

place,' says Spencer. 'Keep your head down, in case they come after you.'

Lottie crouches down next to me. 'Don't you go givin' up, Milly. Between us, we'll prove 'em wrong. Look, you can take this wiv you.'

Lottie pulls a strap over her head. When I see Mum's red velvet evening bag, something sparks inside me. 'I've put Tom's doobries inside, in case you need them.'

I jump up and look through the bag. 'Mum left clues, didn't she? She left the programme. There might be something else I've missed. And Lottie – you need to find her bracelet. That might be able to tell us something too.'

'If it's in Madame's study, we'll find it.'

Spencer nods at Lottie. 'OK, Shorty, we'd better get back before they guess something's up. Merv – don't forget which tunnel to take.'

Lottie gives me a hug, then she and Spencer dash back to the spiral staircase. Spencer pauses on the bottom rung. 'Kydd, I don't suppose it matters now, but you were brilliant tonight. Pity you can't dance tomorrow. We'd have won the Scarlet Slipper for sure.'

'*For sure . . . for sure . . . for sure . . .*' echoes the tunnel as his footsteps clang up the steps.

Merv sniffs next to me.

'So which way now, Merv?'

'We're not going anywhere until you tell me where you hid MUMB. In case, you know, you die or something.'

'Merv, I don't believe you sometimes. Your MUMB's just a *stupid little gadget* but mine's a *real live human being*. Please can we hurry!'

'MUMB means everything to me. I thought you understood.'

'Well, I don't.'

The sound of Merv's sigh echoes down the tunnel.

'OK. It's in the dorm. In my trunk.'

'You call that a hiding place?'

'They won't find it,' I say. 'It's in an old *pointe* shoe, buried in the box. I sewed it up and everything.'

Merv's monobrow does a little Mexican wave. 'Oh. That's OK then.' Then he's off, shuffling down the tunnel, muttering to himself, 'Left, right. No – right, left . . . this would be so much easier with GPS . . .'

He's still muttering as he hurries me along another secret tunnel and up another secret staircase. When we reach the top, my nose twitches. We appear to have surfaced in a cupboard. A dark, stinky cupboard stacked with shelves. I kick over a vegetable rack. Squeeze past a line of jars. We stumble into a steamy kitchen.

Merv doesn't see Cook until it's too late. Her saucepan clangs across the floor. A puddle of grey frogspawn splatters at her feet. 'My semolina!'

Merv pulls on his white mask.

'Sorry, Cook,' I say.

'Oh, it's *you*, Milly!' She tucks her hair into her hairnet. 'You scared the stuffing out of me! Who's *that*? He doesn't look like a ballet dancer.'

'I know,' I say. 'His skills are cerebral.'

'Poor love,' says Cook.

Merv pulls down his mask and speaks in a very deep voice. 'My apologies, Mrs Topping, but may I remind you, we are now in *operation mode*. You know what that means, don't you?'

Cook zips her lips with her finger.

Merv shoves me out of the back door and into the snow. 'Just saying that out loud hurt. I need to lie down.'

The cold cuts through my tutu and tights. 'Were we s-supposed to end up in the k-kitchen?'

'Must have gone left then right, not right then left.'

'But how am I g-going to g-get home from here?'

'It's OK. I've just remembered something else I forgot.' Merv unpadlocks his satchel. 'I've got this.'

He pulls out something that looks suspiciously like a tutu.

'A tutu? How's that going to get me home?'

'Put it on,' says Merv. 'You'll see.'

The tutu is midnight-blue. Merv shakes it at me and silver stars twinkle in a cloud of netting. 'Merv, it's minus two. It's very pretty, but I'm not undressing.'

'Kydd, I went to GREAT LENGTHS to steal this from Madge. She's got more eyes than "impossibilification" and that's got six. And anyway, it's the only way.'

'OK. Don't look.'

I swap my Lilac Fairy tutu for Madge's. Merv's still got his eyes closed as he helps me do it up. 'Can't you keep still for one second?'

'I can't help shaking, Merv. It's not like I'm doing it on purpose.' I pull Mum's evening bag across my shoulders.

'Careful,' says Merv. 'The skirt is constructed of blades.'

'*Blades?*'

'Blades,' says Merv, like this is perfectly normal. 'Rotor blades. Engineered to work in a similar way to the blades of the Popovs' helicopter. But these are fixed to the steel hoops of your tutu and made of advanced carbon fibre. That's a lightweight material used in—'

'Sorry Merv, you lost me at helicopter.'

The refectory lights flicker. 'Hurry up, Kydd. It won't be long before they realize you're missing.'

'But Merv, I DON'T KNOW HOW TO FLY A HELICOPTER!'

'You don't need to. Trust me, I've programmed it to take you to the Bombardier's house.' Merv hits the ignition.

I start to vibrate. 'Garghhh . . .'

'Keep your arms folded!' shouts Merv.

I hug my arms around me as the skirt of my tutu unfolds. Layers of blades begin to turn. They spin faster and faster.

My toes leave the ground. Bit by bit, my tutu whirrs me up in the air.

'DON'T LOOK DOWN!' shouts Merv.

I don't need the warning. I wouldn't look down if Superman flew past – I wouldn't look down if Merv flew past in his underpants. I feel as small and fragile as a snowflake.

Up and up I jerk.

Up and up until my nose is runny.

Up and up until my eardrums pop.

Up and up until my eyeballs ache.

The wind takes me in its grasp. It spins me forward, back, and side to side. I swerve right, over Buckingham Palace. Left, over the Thames. London twinkles like a winter wonderland. It's the most discombobulated I've ever been.

Just when I think I'm going to freeze to death, there's another jerk, and I start to descend. But something's wrong. This isn't Grafton Street. My tutu shudders as I near the ground. The blades slow to a tick. They fold back into the skirt. The gap between me and the ground shrinks to nothing. I hit the snow with a *thwump* and my knees buckle under me.

Headlights blink on the other side of the common. I stagger to my feet, arrange me and my tutu into a more dignified position, and make my way home.

26

The Three Hundred and Fifty-ninth Day with No Mum

I run as fast as I can, which by this point in the evening is not very fast at all. Not only are my legs as wobbly as Cook's Christmas trifle, but the pavement is getting more slippery by the second. I hike up my tutu and manage to only fall over once.

I end up zig-zagging through the side streets and darting from one doorway to the next until I reach the lane at the bottom of our back garden. I know Merv told me to go straight to the Bombardier's, but I'm aching to be home. Plus, I really need a jumper. Climbing over the garden wall isn't as easy as it looks and I drop to the other side with a bit of a crash.

The reflection in the kitchen door is alarming. The Lilac Fairy has gone. In her place is the wicked fairy. My hair is vertical, my nose is red, my tights are holier than a Christmas carol. Poor Madge's flying tutu is in shreds.

I twiddle one of her bobby pins in the lock and, hey presto, it opens.

There's not much call for jumpers in Buenos Aires at this time of year, so luckily there are lots in Bab's wardrobe. My fingertips are too numb to feel for the softest one, so I grab the nearest and pull it over my head. Gratefully, I peel off my ballet shoes and sink against the row of squishy fake fur. I close my eyes and breathe in Bab's smell. I'll just give myself five minutes . . .

I wake up to the sound of a bell. Light leaks through the curtains.

Nooo. I shoot up in a panic, my broken heart galloping like a lame horse. How could I have fallen asleep?

'Oh, it's you, Milly,' says the Bombardier when I answer the door. 'Saw the light on last night and thought your grandmother'd got fed up of all that foreign food and come home early. Place has been very dull without her.' He clears his throat. 'Shouldn't you be in school?'

'I, um, hurt my ankle,' I fib. 'So they let me come home early.'

There's a mew between the Bombardier's legs. A

furry ginger tail brushes my shin.

I scoop Boris up and cover him in kisses. 'Thanks for taking care of him.'

'No problem at all. The old boy ignored me and I ignored him. Perfectly amicable arrangement. Actually, now that you're home, I have something for you.'

The Bombardier rummages around in the pocket of his tweed jacket.

'Chap from Scotland Yard called by a couple of weeks ago. Said a cleaner from the Opera House had been caught pilfering things from lost property. He thought these might be your mother's.'

The Bombardier hands me a little brown paper bag. 'Call in if you need anything, won't you? Happy to share a tin of minestrone, what?'

'Thanks, Bombardier.'

'And tell Catherine her old Villy's looking forward to seeing her. Place has been dull without her. Jolly dull . . .'

Boris waits for me to sit at the kitchen table, then curls next to my feet. I empty the bag and out tumbles a silver charm. I gasp. It's the little ballerina from Mum's bracelet. But the bag's not empty. Inside are two more charms I hadn't even realized were missing. A ballet shoe and a crown.

I line them up in front of me. A ballerina, a ballet shoe and a crown.

Mum must have dropped them on purpose. She was trying to tell me something, but what?

A ballerina. A ballet shoe. A crown.

My brain leaps to its little brain feet.

Boris rolls over as I push my chair away. Upstairs, my ballet shoes are still where I left them. I bring them down and inspect the sole.

The maker's mark is a small, black crown.

A ballerina. A ballet shoe. A crown.

Crown Maker.

The crown Mum drew in the programme had nothing to do with Korolev. She was trying to tell us something about Crown Maker.

But Mr Stubbs never mentioned a Crown Maker.

Boris slinks away and I watch his ginger tail disappear through the cat flap. A draught creeps up my neck and breathes in my ear.

Crown Maker made these shoes.

Crown Maker is Pip.

I have to go to Meekes.

I pull on Bab's coat, jab Madge's bobby pins in my hair and fling the bag across my shoulders. What is Pip up to? What's *Crown Maker* up to?

He might be dangerous. Very.

As the Tube rattles along the Northern Line, I try and fit the pieces together. Mum must have seen Pip on the night she vanished. But Pip's always so nice . . .

The Tube judders to a stop and I *jeté* from the carriage.

I emerge, blinking, into Covent Garden. The streets are strung with fairy lights. A jingle of Christmas songs escapes every doorway. I fight a Yuletide of shoppers and a rising sense of panic.

Did Mr Stubbs fall down the stairs, or was he pushed? Something tells me Edwina Meekes's poltergeist had nothing to with the accidents in Meekes.

I reach the shop and spot a sign stuck inside the misty window.

DUE TO THE SCARLET SLIPPER BALLET PRIZE
AND THE CHRISTMAS HOLIDAYS, MEEKES WILL
BE CLOSED TO THE PUBLIC FOR TWO WEEKS. WE
WOULD LIKE TO WISH THE THREE SCHOOLS
COMPETING THE VERY BEST OF LUCK.

I pause to summon my inner lion but only find a trembling kitten. When I press my nose against the glass, it's dark inside. No Mrs Huntley-Palmer and no shoemakers. It's not easy to twiddle a bobby pin with jittery fingers, but eventually the door tinkles open and I step inside.

The shop smells of silence and secrets. I figure if

there are clues to be found they'll be on Pip's bench. Creak by creak I tiptoe down the staircase to the basement, and feel my way into Pip's nook under the stairs.

In my pocket is Madge's compact. I flip it open and wave the light across the bench. A pair of discarded *pointe* shoes lie on their side. Stamped on the soles under Willow's initials are small black crowns. I tug on the drawer. It's locked. I pull another bobby pin from my hair. When the drawer slides open, a Siberian chill runs down my neck.

Lying underneath an old newspaper is Mum's bracelet.

How did it get here? Did Pip take it from Madame's study? Did *Pip* smash Madame's cabinet?

There's nothing else in the drawer. I pop the bracelet in my bag and grope my way to Mr Stubbs's bench. No clues there either. What should I do now? Go to Swan House? Tell Ms Celia what I know? But what *do* I know? All I've got are three charms and an old programme. That's not proof of anything. I need to find Pip. I need to find Crown Maker.

There's a scratching sound in the darkness. Little claws on the wooden boards. Mice . . . rats? I pause. There's something else too. Not a scratch, or a squeak – a *moan*.

My skin bristles. My nose twitches. My ears flap

like a baby elephant's.

Edwina Meekes's ghost . . .

I dodge the benches, trip down a step and find myself weaving around a room of sleeping sewing machines. At the back, another door leads down a narrow corridor. Summoning all of my pluck, I creep towards the sound. At the end of the corridor is a small musty room with a chair, a table and a desk lamp draped in cobwebs. Against the far wall is a big, black cupboard.

The moaning stops.

I pause before fumbling with the heavy brass latch. When I throw open the door, a roll of satin thumps to the floor in a cloud of dust. My heart thumps with it. I shine the light inside the cupboard and sneeze. Nothing inside but a dead moth with broken wings.

But the sound came from this room, I'm sure of it.

I look up at the ceiling. Down at the floor. Under my feet are flagstones and a rusty metal grate covering an old drain.

The light from the compact wiggles through the grate. When it falls on a silhouette below, I learn a valuable lesson. Screaming is impossible when you are genuinely scared out of your wits.

'Drone on,' I say in a squeaky whisper. The compact begins to whirr. 'Go down,' I say. It hovers over the drain, then rolls to its side and slips through the grate.

Light spills through the gap. My hand flies to my mouth. Gazing up are the biggest, sparkliest eyes I've ever seen.

My fingers squeeze through the gap. My voice squeezes through too.

'Mum? Is that you?'

The woman shakes off the rope around her wrists and tears the tape from her mouth.

Her voice conjures up bedtime stories and scarlet slippers. 'Milly, it *can't* be.'

'Mum!'

'I thought you were *him*! He doesn't know I can free my hands. Oh, Milly!'

'Clever girl,' says Mum, when I explain how I found her. 'But you've got to get out of here, sweetheart. He'll be back at any second.'

I press my face against the grate. 'You mean Pip, don't you? Why's he done this to you?'

Mum is on tiptoes, just out of reach. 'His real name is Filipp Popov. He kidnapped me on the night of the Scarlet Slippers. Oh, Milly. He said he'd kill you if I didn't help him.'

'Say that again – I thought you said *Filipp Popov*?'

'Yes, darling. Pip is Filipp. I'll explain everything later. But now you have to run or he'll kill us both.'

I sit back on my heels. Filipp Popov with the mousey hair and mousey teeth is *Pip*.

'How can that be? Why didn't I see it?'

'No one recognized him, sweetheart. It's not your fault.'

I shake my head. It doesn't make sense, unless . . . 'Does Pip have anything to do with the mole?'

'I don't know, darling. I was gathering evidence, but it was encrypted. I didn't get the chance to pass it on to Swan House.'

I tug on the bars. 'Mum, I'm not leaving without you. There must be some way I can get you out.'

'It's impossible, Milly. The old cellar was bricked up years ago. The only way in and out is through the grate . . .'

'I'll find something! Meekes is full of tools.' I tear back through the narrow corridor and start tugging on drawers.

'It's no good,' Mum calls. 'Filipp's thought of everything. He took all the tools away.'

I scrabble through drawer after drawer but all I find are thimbles and thread.

I run back. 'I'm sorry, Mum. We have to think of something else.'

'It's all right, sweetheart. Don't get upset. You wouldn't have been able to open it anyway. Filipp bolted down the grate when I tried to escape. Then he punished me by sending you that dreadful chocolate shoe. Thank God you didn't eat it.'

'It was *Pip* who gave me the poisoned chocolate? Why does he hate us so much, Mum?'

'It's not just *us*, sweetheart. He hates his family, Swan House, the entire ballet world. He had two left feet, you see. Imagine being the only Popov who couldn't dance. His mother hid him away and treated him dreadfully.'

No wonder he destroyed the Popov cabinet.

'When he failed to win a Scarlet Slipper he went quite mad. He ran away and changed his identity. He persuaded Korolev to take him on before coming back to London. Goodness knows what he learnt in Casova, and now he intends to dance in the Scarlet Slippers . . . Milly, when are they?'

'You don't know? The final dances are tonight.'

'*Tonight?*' Mum's eyes widen. She reaches up. Her fingers are so, so close to mine. 'Milly, listen carefully – he said he was going to plant a bomb. He said he was going to blow up everyone who'd rejected him. Oh, sweetheart, he said he was going to take his revenge on the last night of the competition. You've got to— No, *wait*!' Mum's voice thickens. 'It's too late!'

The bell upstairs tinkles. 'Drone off,' says Mum as she fumbles with the rope. Everything goes black. She whispers through the darkness. 'Quickly, Milly, hide under the table. And don't make a sound.'

Mum reapplies her tape and I crawl under the table. The staircase creaks. Footsteps pad along the workshop. I peek between the table legs and even though my stomach is empty, it wants to be sick.

Lying next to the cupboard is a bright-red roll of satin.

27

The Dying Swan

I hold my breath as Filipp's shadow stretches across the flagstone floor. One step further and he's bound to see the satin lying where it shouldn't be. I may as well be waving a flag. *Here I am. Come and kill me!*

A noise from behind him makes me jump so hard I almost bang my head on the table.

It's an old-fashioned telephone.

Filipp pauses. He sighs. He turns around.

I breathe out and listen as Filipp says, 'Hello, Meekes the Shoemaker's,' in a friendly Pip voice.

While I've got the chance, I scramble between the table legs, heave the roll of satin back into the cupboard then dive back under the table.

Filipp is still chatting. 'Yes, Mrs Huntley-Palmer, I've delivered the Scarlet Slipper trophy. Like I said, you can trust me to lock up for the holidays. You too,

Mrs Huntley-Palmer. Happy Christmas.'

If I could reach the telephone, I could ring for help. But the slam of the receiver is followed by a snip, like the cutting of a phone line.

Seconds later, he's back. Filipp pauses in the doorway, then crouches down.

I press hard against the wall and make myself as small as possible. Filipp kneels on the floor and whines through the grate.

'Is anyone home?'

Mum moans.

'Sorry? What was that, Eva? Did I have a good day? I *did*, thank you for asking. I've spent quite a lot of it wondering what to do with you, actually. But we'll get to that in a second.'

Filipp gets up and shrugs off his overall. Underneath is a shiny black leotard. He reaches for a cape hanging behind the door. Feathers rustle as he pulls it around his neck.

'You'll be pleased to know that my final delivery to Swan House is done and everything has gone to plan. Who would have thought it, eh? Stupid old Filipp pulling off the crime of the century!'

Mum mumbles through the tape and Filipp holds up his palm.

'You thought I was stupid too, Eva. Don't deny it. *Hlúpy*, they called me in Korolev's academy. Stupid

Vilppu, but there's a reason for everything I've done . . .'

Filipp bangs the case on the table above my head. The lock snaps open. He drags back the chair and sits down. He's so close, the smell of glue on his overalls makes my stomach heave again. Something flops to the floor and Filipp kicks it under the table. It looks like a squashed hamster – it's Pip's ginger wig.

Filipp whines on. 'Korolev did me a favour by throwing me out. He forced me to put my plan into action. It was so easy to get a job at Meekes. Young Master Pip. So eager to learn. And I learnt a lot but it was a stroke of luck when you showed up that day. I realized that if *you* taught me, I'd get better. If *you* taught me, I might win a Scarlet Slipper! It took a few attempts to finish Heart Maker off, but it was worth it. You should have seen the look on his face when nice young Pip Smith pushed him down the stairs. He couldn't *Adam and Eve* it . . .'

I clamp my hands over my mouth. Poor Mr Stubbs.

'But look at Pip now, Eva. Look at *Filipp*. Look at CROWN MAKER!'

Mum groans through the tape.

'I'm glad you agree. Anyway, that's enough about me. Let's talk about you. The truth is, I'm torn. Will it be an encore for you, or curtains? I think you've had enough encores, don't you? Meekes is closed for two weeks. With no water, I give you three days.'

Pip scrapes back the chair and stands up. 'I wish you could see me, Eva. I will be the greatest Von Rothbart that has ever danced!' He steps back and swishes his cape.

I crane my neck, but all I can see is a pair of black legs.

'Goodbye, Eva. I will miss our little chats. In some ways you were the m-mother I always hoped for. Don't try to escape, will you? If anyone tries to stop me, I have something up my sleeve. One wrong move, and I'll press this little button. So, you see, there really is nothing you can do. Toodle *Pip* – *Filipp* has an appointment with revenge.'

He steps inside the cupboard. There's a creak and a clang, then silence.

I wait a heartbeat before wriggling from under the table. 'There must be a tunnel from Meekes all the way to Swan House.'

Mum pulls off the tape. 'You know about the tunnels? Even I didn't realize there was one to Meekes. You must hurry. The remote control is in his sleeve, but I don't know where he's planted the bomb. Poor Filipp – he wants so desperately to win a Scarlet Slipper. I don't believe he'll detonate the bomb until after he's danced. You have to follow him, Milly, then get help.'

'I'll come back for you, Mum. As soon as I can.'

'Stay safe. Milly, I love you . . .'

'I love you too, Mum.'

I run with gulping breaths and heavy legs. An invisible string tugs me back to Mum but Filipp's feet are thumping away. His words swoop over my head like angry bats.

'*Sssscarlet Sssslipper . . . Po-po-va*, *Po-po-va . . .*'

I scrape my arms and stub my toes. I run until my legs give up. I think of Mum and run some more. I run until Filipp slows.

In front of him, a staircase spirals up into the dark. His footsteps clang above my head. I climb as quiet as a see-through mouse.

There's a muffled chime as he disappears through a crack of light. I scramble after him and peer through a narrow door. The grandfather clock. I'm back where I started.

A boy calls into Madame's study, 'Are you there, Pip?' I know that voice. It's Danny Debello. My brain ticks in time with the clock. Danny is dancing the part of Von Rothbart. 'Hi, Pip. Thanks for coming back,' says Danny. 'Just as well you got here in time.

Like I said on the phone, the shoes you dropped off with the trophy were way too big. Wait a minute – *what's going—?*'

There's a thump and a slump. I watch Filipp step over Danny's legs and run.

I wriggle out of the clock and check that Danny's breathing. He's alive, but his Von Rothbart mask has gone. Filipp must be planning to take his place.

As I pull myself up, a shadow falls over me.

'Millicent! What have you done?'

Moonlight pours from the window. Madame looks like she's made of snow.

'Madame, this isn't how it looks! It was Pip! He's going to blow up the theatre. You have to warn everyone!'

Madame checks Danny's pulse. 'First you disappear, zen you attack Daniel and now you expect me to believe zat *Pip* is planning to blow us all up? Even by your standards, zat is *ridicule*!'

'I'm telling the truth! I found Mum at Meekes. Pip had her all along!'

'You found Eva?' Madame drops Danny's wrist.

'YES! She's not the mole. I haven't got time to explain but you've got to send someone for her, and I've got to stop—'

'*You* are going nowhere. I will call ze Captain.'

'NO! LISTEN TO ME! Pip is Filipp Popov.'

'Filipp Popov? You know zis?'

'He's going to take revenge on his family. Please, Madame, you must warn everyone.'

'I don't believe you.'

'What if you're wrong? Hundreds of people will die. Can you take that chance?'

Madame melts into the unlit hall. 'Go,' she says. 'I will raise the alarm.'

The hall is quiet. Everyone must be in the theatre. I dart into the narrow corridor that leads backstage. There's only one person who can stop Filipp now.

I find the White Swan stretching in the shadows. Willow looks up and her jaw drops open.

'You're not supposed to be here. I'm calling Madame. Madame! MADAME! It's Mil—'

I clamp my hand over Willow's kale 'ole. 'Sorry, Willow. Have you seen Von Rothbart? Is he in the wings? Just nod or shake your head.'

Willow nods.

'I need you to listen very carefully. Von Rothbart is *not* Danny. I don't have time to explain, but he's planted a bomb in the theatre. I'm going to take my hand away now. Do you promise not to shout?'

Willow nods. I drop my hand.

'You're off your tiny rocker! MADAME! MILLICENT'S G—'

Oh, for goodness' sake. My hand slaps back over

Willow's mouth.

'Please, *please*, listen. He's carrying a remote control. He won't use it until after he's danced. You have to get it off him before the dance ends. Do you understand? You have to get the control.'

I take my hand away and Willow crumbles.

'He's got a bomb?'

'Yes.'

'And you want me to dance with him?'

'Yes.' I grab her hand.

'NO WAY! Milly, I can't do it. I'm too pretty to die.'

Willow is shaking. Her violet eyes are pools of terror. Her hand is hot and trembly. It's like *Cinderella* all over again.

I let her go. 'I'm sorry, Willow. I should never have asked you. Quick, give me your mask – your costume . . .'

Willow peels off her mask. 'It's too dangerous, Milly. You can't.'

I make my voice as light as a little white feather. 'It's OK. I've warned Madame. They might have found the bomb by now.'

Willow takes off her costume. She helps me into the tutu. Lastly, I put on her shoes. When I see Mum's initials on the soles, invisible fingers tickle my neck. Suddenly everything becomes clear.

Filipp said it himself, he did everything for a reason. He became a shoemaker *because* of the Scarlet Slipper. If I can hide Merv's MUMB in the box of a ballet shoe, wouldn't it be possible for Filipp to hide a bomb in the trophy? Isn't that why he pushed Mr Stubbs down the stairs – so *he* could make the Scarlet Slipper?

'Tell the Captain the bomb must be inside the trophy. What are you waiting for? Go!'

Willow folds her arms. 'If you're going to die, I have to say something first.'

'We haven't got time!'

'I'm not going until I've said it! After I hurt my leg in *Cinderella*, one little lie led to another and I just couldn't stop. Dad was always working and your mum was the first person to take an interest in me and my dancing. She was so amazing and kind, I didn't *want* to stop. I was scared that if I changed my story she wouldn't want anything to do with me.' Willow Perkins rolls her eyes. 'What I mean is, I'm sorry, Milly. There, I said it.'

I watch her scarper down the corridor. All this time I've been jealous of Willow, but I had the one thing she wanted all along. A mum.

28

The Final Act

I wobble up the steps to the wings with a heart that's three sizes too big for my bodice. Von Rothbart's winged cape swooshes in front of me. The air crackles. A voice onstage warbles, 'Your Royal Majesties, my Lords, Ladies and Gentlemen, esteemed Judges and Committee Members. It is my great pleasure to introduce . . .'

It's Dame Anna Popova. Doesn't she want to live to be 103? Why hasn't the Captain cleared the theatre? What has Madame been *doing*?

I listen for the alarm but the only warning bells are the ones going off in my brain.

Madame hasn't told the Captain about the bomb. Madame hasn't told anyone about the bomb. Madame is nowhere to be seen.

Madame is the MOLE.

Suddenly there's a frozen lake where my stomach

should be. If I don't stop Filipp, no one will.

Every cell in my body zooms in on one thing. The remote control in Filipp's sleeve.

I edge as close as I dare to his back and peer around the curtain. Up in the Royal Box, the Scarlet Slipper gleams in front of Filipp's mum.

I watch him watch Dame Anna as she nudges her glasses up her powdery nose.

' . . . we have a surprise, thanks to Madame de La Cloche's wonderful suggestion . . .'

A surprise?

The backdrop grates behind me. Slowly, it begins to rise. There's a blast of cold air. Moonlight fills the stage. Filipp's eyes slide from Dame Anna to his mother, to the icy lake. Stars twinkle above and below the horizon. We're in a snowglobe of starlight. A globe that'll explode into a shower of glittering dust if I fail.

Dame Anna Popova's voice warbles into a crescendo. ' . . . from *Swan Lake*, I give you . . . SWAN HOUSE SCHOOL OF BALLET!'

The clapping dies. The lights dim. Silence falls over the theatre like stardust.

Filipp said we perform, or we die. But I don't need to perform. I *am* Odette. A frightened White Swan, on the verge of doom.

The conductor lifts his baton. The baton comes

down. Music floods my ears.

Filipp soars across the stage like a bird. He preens, he glares, he leaps, he flaps. Symbols clash as he sweeps me up and spins me around. I throw back my arms and feathers fly. For a heartbeat, I'm lost in the music. It flows through my arms and legs. It sparks from my fingertips, it shines in my eyes.

Ms Celia said that miracles could only be achieved with patience and kindness and Mum has proved her right. The audience don't wait for the final drum roll, they jump to their feet and applause thunders around us. In the corner of my eye, I spot the Captain enter the Royal Box. As Filipp takes a long, low bow, I sidestep closer and reach out my hand. At that second, Filipp looks up. He snaps out of his trance and reaches for his sleeve.

I think of Lottie as I make a claw and pounce. Filipp prods a scratch on his cheek and inspects the blood on his fingertip.

For an instant, I see the young Filipp with his slumpy shoulders and mousey ears. I grab his sleeve and feel the remote. He twists my arm. I jab with my elbow. He lets go and the remote slides into my hand.

I roll away, but he clings to my tutu and drags me back. My palms are too slippery. The remote spins out of my grasp. I kick it towards the lake and watch it teeter at the edge of the stage. I pray for a splash that doesn't come. We both lurch towards it but Filipp catches my ankle. I feel a horrible snap and I cry out. Blurry eyed, I dive again, but he's already there.

'Don't,' I choke. 'Don't. You've won the Scarlet Slipper.'

For a second, he falters. Then, eyes on his mother, Filipp Popov laughs and presses the button.

I curl up. Hands on ears. Cheeks wet hot. *Mum, I've let you down . . .*

And . . . nothing.

I open one eye. Then the other. Above me, the royals are all staring at the white face of the Captain. His eyes are screwed shut. His Viking arms are hugging his Viking chest. The trophy is stuffed up his jumper. The Captain is a viking god. But why hasn't the trophy exploded?

The audience begins to rustle. Some of them check their programmes. They must think this is part of the performance. Everyone settles back in their seats.

Well. Not quite everyone.

At the back of the theatre, no one seems to have noticed a boy puffing like Thomas the Tank Engine. He's got headphones over his ears and his monobrow is a bushy black line of concentration. His outstretched hand trembles at the stage then he slides MUMB into his satchel, locks the padlock and heads back to the control room.

Merv Crump. He doesn't know how special he is.

Behind me, there's a roar. Filipp shakes the remote. I pull myself up and, with one last effort, *grand jeté* into his chest. The only sound as we topple off the edge of the stage is Topsy's cry of 'ENCORE!'

The lake snatches my breath away. Filipp swims towards a black shape in the water. The moon appears from behind the clouds and a boat emerges. *L'Odette*. An engine splutters and the sound vibrates across the lake. Filipp's going to get away. He must have planned it all along; a fiery explosion and a watery escape.

And me? I've gone from the frying pan into the freezer. I try to swim after him, but my legs won't work. My chest is all ice and no air.

I ache with cold. I'm numb with it. And I'm so very . . .

. . . very . . .

. . . sleepy . . .

'MILLY!'

A soggy hot-water bottle bobs under my chin.

'Hang on to Boris!' yells Lottie.

Boris? I feel hands under my arms.

'Lottie – you've got to rescue Mum,' I wheeze. 'She's in Meekes.'

'Don't worry,' says Lottie as she and Spencer tug me into the boat. 'We won't let anyfink bad happen to her.'

'Unlike him . . .' adds Spencer.

Filipp is slumped over the wheel of the boat.

'*I* stopped him wiv my Tiger Claw,' says Lottie.

'Because *I* told you he was going to use the boat,' says Spencer.

Lottie punches Spencer on the arm. 'Milly's the one we should be fanking.'

'And Merv,' I say. 'If it wasn't for Merv, we'd be toast.'

'Teamwork,' says Spencer.

'Teamwork,' says Lottie.

'Teamwork,' I say.

'You know what . . . ?' says Lottie.

But I don't hear the rest.

I think I take a little nap.

29

The Scarlet Slipper

When I wake up, I have no idea where I am. Buttery sunlight spills across the bedspread. I sit upright and a damp, ginger hot-water bottle slides off my cheek.

I've got my hot-water bottle Boris back but where's Mum?

Nurse bustles into the infirmary. 'Oh, good. You're awake. You've got a queue in the waiting room, you know. I've told them they can't all come in at once.'

'Is my mum out there?'

Nurse shakes her head. I leap out of bed and my ankle screams.

Nurse tucks me back under the covers. 'You're not going anywhere, young lady.'

'But my mum—'

'No need to panic.' Nurse draws back the curtain

of the bed next to me. 'Your mum is right here.'

Mum is fast asleep. There are lines on her face I don't remember and her brow is slightly furrowed, as if she's trying to solve a puzzle in her dreams. But twelve months on, she's as lovely as ever.

Nurse snaps the curtain shut. 'We've given her a sedative. Poor, brave lady was exhausted with worry, and she still managed to spend half the night talking with Ms Celia. She'll wake up in a couple of hours.'

There's a tap on the door. 'Can we come in?' says a no-nonsense voice.

'Don't come any closer!' I grab the nearest thing on the trolley next to me, which happens to be a toothbrush. After everything that's happened, I am understandably suspicious of Ms Celia and the Captain. 'This isn't what you think it is. It's one of Madge's doobries and it's loaded!'

Ms Celia hides a smile. 'We know Eva isn't the mole, Milly. We made a mistake. *I* made a mistake.' She draws up a chair between the beds and takes my hand. 'I'm so very, very sorry.'

The Captain stands at the end of the bed. 'The real mole was caught on her way to Meekes.'

'You arrested Madame?'

'Yes,' says Ms Celia. 'Fortunately we found her before she found Eva.'

'She was going to hurt Mum?'

'She thought Eva knew she was the mole. She's not talking yet, but luckily we have all the evidence we need on this.' Ms Celia holds out a charm from Mum's bracelet. A silver swan covered in diamonds. She twists the neck and it comes apart. 'It's your mother's memory stick. It contains all the information she managed to download from Korolev's computer. The moment Madame saw it, she guessed what was on it. Madame wasn't sure how much you knew, so she used Willow to keep an eye on you. Willow didn't know why, but she was only too happy to oblige.'

'But why did Madame change sides?'

'She didn't,' says the Captain.

'What do you mean?'

'It appears Madame has been on Korolev's side from the beginning,' says Ms Celia. 'They had one thing in common – a desperate ambition to win the Scarlet Slipper. *Madame* was the mastermind behind the poisoning when they were students and Korolev took the blame. I should have seen the signs . . .'

'You couldn't have known, Celia,' says the Captain.

'I knew how much Blanche coveted a Scarlet Slipper, and how jealous she was of Eva. She was obsessed with the White Swan. Look at the way she dressed – even her room was white, for heaven's sake.'

The Captain shuffles his Viking feet. 'Blanche deceived us all.'

'Thank you, Garth, but I won't forgive myself that easily.'

'Was Madame helping Filipp too?' I ask.

Ms Celia shakes her head. 'Filipp Popov discovered she was a mole when he was a student in Korolev's academy. He blackmailed her to help him take part in the competition.'

'So all those times Pip came here with deliveries, he was putting pressure on Madame. Did she know about the bomb?'

'We think he kept that to himself, although he must have asked Madame to make sure the back of the stage was open.'

'But I still don't see where Korolev fits in to all this. Did he know what Filipp was up to?'

Ms Celia sighs. 'We don't believe he did. All Korolev wanted was a Scarlet Slipper. He knew nothing of Filipp's plot.'

I think back to the photograph of the Popovs. The lonely little boy in the upstairs window. 'What will happen to Filipp now? Will he go to prison?'

'Sorry, pet,' says the Captain quietly. 'Popov fooled Spencer and Li into thinking he was unconscious, but while you were being lifted out of the boat, he jumped in the lake. We're looking for him now, but as you know, he wouldn't have lasted five minutes in those temperatures.'

'Poor Filipp. I can't help feeling sorry for him.'

'Dame Anna is very upset,' says Ms Celia. 'She thought she saw Filipp at the competition last year, and she was right. Moments later, he kidnapped your mother.'

'Eva's lucky to have you,' says the Captain. 'You showed a lot of pluck last night.'

'And you danced beautifully,' says Ms Celia. '*Cycni venustas, cor leonis*. We all owe you our lives.'

'I couldn't have done it without Merv,' I say.

'He's in the waiting room now. Your friends have something rather special to give you. By the way, Milly, only the four of you know O's real identity. I would remind you of that old Russian proverb – *boltuna yazyk do dobra ne dovede*.'

'A fool's tongue runs before his feet?'

'Indeed. It is vitally important that your mother's continued involvement with the school remains top secret. Do you understand?'

I nod as Ms Celia draws herself up. 'Good girl. Happy Christmas, Milly, we hope to see you back next term.'

The Captain winks and wraps a postbox-red scarf around his Viking neck. 'Our best students are always the ones who prove us wrong. Well done, Kydd.'

There are voices outside the infirmary. 'All right, all right. You can come in now,' says Nurse. 'But keep the noise down. Milly's mum needs her rest.'

'Needs her what?' Spencer dives on the bed.

'Ouch, Spencer!'

Nurse flaps him off with her apron.

'Sorry, Kydd, forgot about the ankle.' He plonks down on the chair and sticks his feet on my blanket.

Lottie bounds in and punches me on the arm. 'You're a legend. Never knew you could do a Tiger Claw!'

I rub my arm. 'Thanks, but it was more of a Boris Claw.'

'Then Boris must be a legend too.' Lottie catches Nurse's eye. 'She'll be all right for next term, won't she, Nurse?'

'*If* she rests over the Christmas holidays.'

'HURRY UP, Merv,' shouts Spencer. 'It's a sprained ankle, not the bubonic plague.'

Nurse shushes at Spencer. 'Last chance, young man.'

'Close your eyes, Milly,' says Lottie as Merv lopes in, wearing his mask.

Something heavy lands on my lap.

'OK. You can open them now.'

I don't know whether to laugh or scream. The last time I saw a Scarlet Slipper trophy it was about to explode.

Spencer grins. 'Don't worry, Kydd. It's a replica.'

'Read what it says!' says Lottie.

I gasp. '*Millicent Kydd, Swan House School of Ballet.*'

Lottie does a little skip. 'We won, Milly! *You* won! The judges said your dancin' blew them away.'

Spencer raises an eyebrow. 'It almost blew them *up*.'

Merv pulls down his mask. 'Can I go now?'

'Wait, Merv, I need to say something. I'm sorry I called your MUMB a silly little gadget.'

'Who's mum?' asks Spencer.

'Can't talk about that,' says Merv.

'Oh, she's *very* special,' I say, smiling at Merv. He hugs his satchel and smiles back. At least, I think he's smiling. It's hard to tell.

'There's something else that's been puzzling me,' I say. 'How did you know Filipp would try to escape in the boat?'

Spencer stretches his long legs and yawns like a lion. 'When Madame told Mr Special to open the back of the stage, he guessed she was up to something. You'd never know it, but Merv's actually quite clever. He asked me to watch the lake, and I don't know what got into me, but I actually did what I was told for once. As soon as I saw the boat had been moved, I called Shorty.'

'Me and my Tiger Claw was waitin' for him!' says Lottie. 'Shame he had to go and escape.'

I put the Scarlet Slipper on the trolley. It's amazing, but not as amazing as my friends.

'Anyway, before I forget, Topsy gave us this to give to you.' Spencer leans over to give me a cellophane bag tied with red ribbon. 'I think it's a memento of our near-death experience.'

Inside are three black biscuity blobs.

'It's gingerbread,' says Lottie. 'S'posed to be *us*. That's me wiv no legs and Merv's the one wiv the satchel. I gave *you* to Danny, I knew you wouldn't mind.'

'He's all right?'

'Yeah. Just feels like an idiot for bein' taken in by Perkins.'

Spencer opens the bag and starts to munch. 'You've got this too.' He hands me an envelope.

Inside is a note written in shaky blue ink.

Dear Miss Millicent. I've said it before and I'll say it again, once a dancer, always a dancer. I'll be back at me Uncle Bob at Meekes just as soon as me knees are fixed. I always knew you was a winner! Congratulations and warmest wishes. Alfred Stubbs.

Next to the name is a little black heart. I slide the

note under my pillow.

Something pings in Spencer's pocket. He pulls out his old phone. 'Got to go and rescue my father from Topsy.' He shakes his head. 'This phone is so last century.'

Nurse comes bustling back. 'OK, you three, say goodbye. There's just one more person who'd like to see you, Milly.'

As everyone leaves, Willow Perkins swans in like nothing's happened. She holds out a bunch of snowdrops. 'I got you these.'

'I . . .' We both speak at once. 'You first,' I say.

Willow puts her hands on her hips and sticks her nose in the air. 'I said I was sorry, and I am. But that doesn't mean I like you.'

'It doesn't mean I like you either,' I say.

Then we both laugh.

Willow puts the flowers in my water glass. 'I don't expect you to understand, but Eva was the closest thing to a mum I had. I don't even love ballet like you do – I just loved the attention. You're so lucky, Milly. She's the kindest person in the world.'

I see that now. Mum helped Filipp. She helped Cook and Topsy when Mr Topping died. And most of all, she helped Willow.

'I do understand, and I'm sorry too.'

'Anyway, I've got to go, my dad's waiting. He just

got engaged. She's taking me to *The Nutcracker* in the holidays.'

'That's great. Happy Christmas, Willow.'

'And you.' She blinks at my hot-water bottle Boris. 'And just so you know, it was Bumble's idea to steal him. She doesn't like cats.' Then Willow Perkins rolls her violet eyes and skips away.

Finally, I can look forward to Christmas with just me and Mum, and maybe Bab if she's had enough tango-ing. As Nurse fusses over my bed, I fight a yawn. The yawn wins and I sink into a deep and dreamless sleep.

When I wake up, someone is stroking my hair. I open my eyes and get squashed into a flannelette nightie. Mum and I hold each other tight. There are no words in English, Russian or Casovan that can describe how lovely it feels. Mum doesn't let me go until we've cried a year's worth of tears and hugged a year's worth of hugs. 'Oh, Milly, I've waited so long to do that.'

'Me too. And I really wish Bab was back.'

'I spoke to her last night. She's on her way. But I can't stay, I'm afraid. I've got somewhere important to go.'

Knowing Mum's a spy doesn't make it any easier to let her go.

'For Christmas?'

Mum nods. I try not to show how disappointed I am. 'I don't suppose you're allowed to tell me where?'

'It is top secret so you must promise not to tell anyone.'

'I promise.'

She whispers in my ear. 'Well, I don't know about you, but I think it's time we both went *home*.'

Acknowledgements

Tragically, my own ballet career went down a plug-hole, age six, but that's another story. This story begins in the Spring of 2013, when Milly and I took a *grand jeté* into the unknown. We'd still be waiting in the wings if it wasn't for some extraordinary people.

I'm so grateful to the very first person to meet Milly, the Golden Egg Academy's Nicki Marshall, who encouraged me to keep writing. Also, if it hadn't been for a brilliant Arvon workshop, I would never have met the amazing folk who gave me the confidence to apply for an MA in Writing for Young People. Enormous thanks to the tutors at Bath Spa University; the fabulous Julia Green, David Almond, Steve Voake, Janine Amos, John McLay, and my mentor, Lucy Christopher – Lucy, I wish you were available in virtual form. Likewise, my wise and wonderful agent, Nicola Barr.

Many years ago, I read an inspirational article in the *Writers' and Artists' Yearbook* by a publisher/wizard by the name of Barry Cunningham. *Ahh*, I thought to myself, *if I was ever to write an actual book, he'd be the first person I'd send it to* . . . huge thanks to Barry, for seeing Milly's potential when she was still very much a pumpkin. Thanks also to Rachel Hickman and Helen Crawford-White for my stunning cover, and to everyone at Chicken House for being so lovely; Rachel Leyshon, Laura Myers, Jazz Bartlett Love, Elinor Bagenal, Sarah Wilson, Lucy Horrocks and Laura Smythe. Extra special Thor-sized thanks to my editor, Kesia Lupo – you picked Milly up, dusted her off and rocketed her to the finale. You are my Lottie, Spencer and Merv rolled into one.

Also untiringly cheering me on and up have been my writing corps and sleepover pals; Julie, Sarah, Kathryn, Kirsty, Maddy, Christina, Finbar, Kita, Zoe, Imogen, Anna and Lynn. You are all exceptional writers and brilliant human beings. Same goes for Jacqui, who was both of those things and more. Heaps of gratitude to Mick, Jeni, Vicky, Sal, Sarah Doobrie, Katie and Chris for your hugs, hurrahs and hot dinners. Thank you for the photos, Chris. A lesser man would have crumbled.

Bottomless love and thanks go to my family. To Paul, Izzy, Gill and Maddy. My gorgeous mum – who was almost certainly a spy – how else could she always have known what I was thinking? My dear dad, who I hear in every story I tell. And Jude, who, despite being forced (i.e. sat on) to read the earliest ramblings of the bossiest sister in all of Wales, still loves me. Most importantly, I couldn't have started or finished Milly's story without my magnificent boys, Rog, Rory and Drew. Rog, you're the Steed to my Purdy . . . the Nureyev to my Fontaine . . .

Which brings me back to ballet. I began by saying that I haven't danced in a very long while. Thanks to Claire Tracey for putting me through my paces and to Sabin Huban for casting her expert eye over Milly's ballet classes. I hope you'll forgive me for taking outrageous liberties with your awe-inspiring world. And lastly, thanks to you, the total star who's *still* reading! You are what dreams are made of. I hope you enjoyed Milly's story and that you'll join her in her next adventure.

Cycni venustas, cor leonis!

Helen Lipscombe

TRY ANOTHER GREAT BOOK FROM CHICKEN HOUSE

THE LAST CHANCE HOTEL by NICKI THORNTON

Seth is the oppressed kitchen boy at the remote Last Chance Hotel, owned by the nasty Bunn family. His only friend is his black cat, Nightshade. But when a strange gathering of magicians arrives for dinner, kindly Dr Thallomius is poisoned by Seth's special dessert. A locked-room murder investigation ensues – and Seth is the main suspect.

The funny thing is, he's innocent . . . can he solve the mystery and clear his name, especially when magic's afoot?

A jolly, atmospheric mystery.
THE TIMES

Hercule Poirot meets Harry Potter in this mind-bending, magical, murder mystery.
MISS CLEVELAND IS READING

Paperback, ISBN 978-1-911077-67-1, £6.99 • ebook, 978-1-911490-41-8, £6.99